ISBN: (paperback) 979-8-9951097-0-9

Printed in the United States of America

Table of Contents

GOBLINS AND CRYSTALS

From the Realms of Lurin Series

An adventurous, regency-inspired fantasy
with a glimmer of romance

Written by

C.A. MEADOWS

For those who wish they had green skin, crave

adventure, and a life on their own terms

Lumiara Mountains

Prologue

Long Ago

The clan of nearly eighty goblins had traveled for far too long, and their muscles ached. They had been hiking through the Lumiara Mountain Range for weeks, searching for new places to build better homes. To the north were the fae, and although they had established a form of peace with them, they didn't want to live alongside them. They had always believed that the fae thought they were better than them. They dressed in finer clothes, kept themselves cleaner, all things that didn't matter to a woodland goblin. The goblins were happiest in nature, among the trees, living off what the land provided. With their skin in all shades of green, they were much easier to blend into their surroundings, further protecting them from harm. They also worried that the fae would attempt to steal their treasures. Their gold. This may seem like a contradiction from their love of nature, and it is that the greedy goblins also loved all things special and shiny.

This was of utmost importance to them. The protection of their materialistic things.

They weren't sure what was to the south, only that another species of magical being lived there, and they weren't willing to find out what that could be.

Eventually, they made their way to the highest point of the largest mountain. So high up that it looked as though you could reach up and grab hold of the moon. Close to the very top, they discovered a cave. With no hesitation, they entered the dark and gloomy hole in the mountain wall. They walked cautiously, as cautiously as a goblin could walk, to be sure not to disturb the mountain. The walls of the cave were lined with sharp, jagged, bright shades of purple and aquamarine colored crystals that glowed under their torches' light. Along with crystals that were solid white and black ones that looked to be filled with stars. They feared any disturbance would send the stones flying and potentially kill them where they stood. The ground beneath their clubbed bare feet was cold and damp, and they could hear the small growls of the tiny dragon-flies they'd encountered along their journey surrounding them. Almost as if they were trying to warn them.

Dragon-flies were, by definition, an invasive species that were heavily hunted and captured. They were sought after for their small size, which could easily penetrate enemy territory without being detected, and their ability to still produce a decent flame. They could fit in the palm of a hand and were all colorful. No two were alike. This was the first encounter the goblins had ever had with these small creatures. Having only heard stories of them and the dangers they bring, they didn't want to make them angry. A swarm of dragon-flies could render their clan useless. However, the goblins knew that it would be better for these pesky creatures to be on their side. So, they would tempt them with treats and safety to ensure their loyalty.

After weeks of scouting, the goblins gaped in awe at the sight of a wondrous cavern. It was nothing as they'd seen before. It was magnificent, magical. They could hear the faint sound of rushing water and hoped that there was a stream they could drink from close by. They were tired and needed rest and nourishment. Their muscles strained to keep them walking. A few of the younger goblins were now being carried by their parents, in straps made from tree roots and vines that held them to their backs. They followed the noise and finally found the small stream coming from the ceiling of the mountain. Flowing its way across the ceiling, down the walls, along the ground, and into a large hole in the wall to their right. They all followed the trail of glistening water, wondering how it was able to flow on the ceiling without dripping down to the ground and where it was coming from.

"Let the women and children rest here. The rest of us will follow the water." King Gibbous of the Goblins announced.

The women all plopped to the ground after helping remove their children from the backs of the men, pulling preserved fruits and meats from their packs to give to the young. All except for the Queen, who insisted that she remain by her husband's side. The female goblins all sat and rubbed their exhausted muscles. The children immediately fell asleep.

The men of King Gibbous' clan followed without question. The water led them to a small tunnel, which opened into a large cavern, and in its center rested a large, glowing crystal, surrounded by the smaller purple, aquamarine, white, and black ones protruding from the walls and ground. The large crystal sat on a heap of dirt in the center of what appeared to be a shallow lake. They watched the water ripple with each drop that came from above. The ceiling had a hole directly above the crystal, giving it its only source of light. The crystal appeared to be clear but was emitting a light blue glow. Their eyes grew wide at the sight, and they all smiled. The crystal's warm glow let off a sense of calm and safety that put all the goblins at ease. After a few moments of basking in the crystal's glory, the crystal began to glow brighter. As it did, the light reflected onto the other, smaller crystals, creating direct beams of light from one to the next. They all suddenly started to feel their strength returning. Not just returning but growing. The tiredness they'd been feeling vanished, and they could see better in the darkness than they had before. The warriors of the group all glanced around at each other in amazement.

"We must preserve this crystal. Protect it." The King proclaimed to his tribe of warriors, not taking his eyes off the magnificent crystal before him.

He approached the crystal cautiously and knelt before it. His knees and legs rested in the cool water. "But how?" One warrior questioned.

Sod was King Gibbous's right hand and was always his voice of reason. The King valued Sod dearly.

"We will move it. We will move it somewhere safe." The warriors nodded and slowly approached the crystal.

The closer they got, the brighter it got, shifting from its dazzling blue to a fierce crimson. One warrior, the bravest of them all, reached out to touch the crystal. As he did, he screamed out in agony. When he pulled his hand back, it was blistered and bright red, with fresh blood coating his palm.

"Leave it. No one else touches it. Where is the healer? Tend to his hand." The King yelled before he sat in the water, staring at the crystal.

The other warriors hurried off with the injured goblin, swiftly moving past Queen Twilight, who had positioned herself in the entryway of the cavern that held the crystal; her sights fixed on her husband. King Gibbous's mind ran a mile a minute trying to figure out a way to protect this crystal. How would he keep it safe, but also ensure that no one else discovered it or was injured in the process?

"We will protect you," King Gibbous whispered to the crystal before standing and turning his attention to his Queen. "My dear Queen Twilight, how would you feel about placing our settlement here, surrounding this crystal? It appears to give us great gifts." King Gibbous asked his Queen.

Queen Twilight nodded her head. "I think that is a wonderful idea. The mountain range is beautiful and full of fresh vegetation. I think it would be a very suitable home. However, we do not know what other creatures reside here. I feel we should find that out before we decide permanently."

The Queen approached and hugged her king before she placed a gentle kiss on his cheek, making the King blush.

"Not in front of everyone." He said shyly before turning to his people. "We will create a wonderful settlement here, in the Lumiara Mountains. We will protect this crystal, and in return, it will grant us strength and better vision." The crowd of goblins cheered before exiting the cave to begin building their dream settlement.

Little did the King know that those wouldn't be the only gifts the crystals would bestow on them. The King and Queen remained with the crystal, still in awe over what they had found. The King placed his arm around the Queen, as she gently rested her hand upon his chest. The crystal then shifted from the crimson red of anger to a light pink, filling both the King and Queen with a feeling of passion. The longer they stood, the pinker it got. The King tilted his head in disbelief. Does this stone have feelings? Does it read ours?

"I believe as long as we remain happily married, the crystal will continue to grant us gifts. We must keep the bloodline going and ensure that there is always a king and queen seated on our thrones. We must lead with dignity, love, and grace to please the crystal. I believe this is what it wants." King Gibbous announced. The Queen eyed him with suspicion.

"Where are you getting these ideas? We know nothing of this crystal. We should have someone investigate it thoroughly."

"Our Maker speaks to me. The crystal speaks to me. It is reading us as much as we are studying it. It changes colors according to its mood," The King replied to his wife, not taking his eyes off the crystal. "I can hear our maker's voice in my head, telling me to be careful. That dabbling with magical objects can be dangerous. I also hear another voice, I believe it's the crystal. It is telling me that we must protect it and keep the bloodline intact. If we do those things, then the crystal will continue to grant us these gifts."

You may call me the Lýsa Crystal. Echoed through King Gibbous's head.

Chapter One

Present Day

As per tradition, all the goblins gathered in the great hall within the largest of the mountains in Lumiara, waiting to hear from the King and Queen about who the Princess would marry. The room was buzzing with anticipation as King Verdant and Queen Moonglade took their places on the royal thrones. The thrones were made of redwood branches with moss cushions and covered with lavender and jasmine flowers that hung gracefully down the back and sides and sprinkled with their own gold dust. The flowers filled the room with a calming scent. They were magnificent and ancient, having been around since the first goblin settlement. The walls of the great hall had been carved with pictures of past Kings and Queens, adorned with gems embedded where their jewelry had once lain on their bodies. Statues littered the sides of the room, all depictions of a time when goblins were honored as heroes. High above them, dangling from the ceiling, hung thousands of crystals that reflected sunlight from giant holes smashed through the mountain's walls, creating windows.

King Verdant escorted Queen Moonglade with pride as they walked arm in arm. Their moss and flower-covered robes trailed behind them. He assisted her into her chair before taking a seat on his own. They were followed by their only daughter, Princess Strelitzia, who took a seat on her father's left in a smaller throne. It was customary for the Queen to sit on the King's right as second in command.

Strelitzia loved these thrones. She had always thought they were beautifully made. The moss had been replaced a few times to maintain a comfort level fit for royalty. As she sat in her smaller throne, she glanced over at the thrones of her parents. Although she was in no rush to be queen, she did envy her parents' larger thrones and was excited at the thought that one day she would sit there.

Once everyone had filed in and was settled, King Verdant rose, ready to speak to his clan.

"Welcome. Today, we ask my daughter who she has chosen to be her King. This is always a monumental moment for us goblins, and I assure you that today will be nothing less. I remember when I chose my Queen," He paused and looked over at Queen Moonglade, smiling, "It was the happiest day of my life, and she had no idea it was coming." The crowd all laughed. "As you all know, this tradition started long before any of us were around. Over one hundred years ago, King Gibbous discovered the Lýsa Crystal and made a deal with it. Today, we please the Lýsa Crystal with the promise of the next marriage of royalty. Ensuring our clan's future and the continuation of the gifts we receive. Everyone, I give you

Princess Strelitzia." King Verdant concluded as he applauded his daughter.

Strelitzia gulped, then took a deep breath as she closed her eyes to steady her racing heart. The crowd cheered while anger and anxiety bubbled inside Princess Strelitzia. King Verdant was right in one aspect: this would be monumental. Strelitzia rose from her chair and made her way to the edge of the platform, facing the crowd, petrified. She knew what they were all waiting for and knew what their reactions would be to her news, and she had felt a ping of anxiety sitting heavily in her stomach. The retaliation, though? That is what she feared. Goblins were always known for their harsh retaliations.

"Hello," The Princess began, and an unnerving hush fell over the room, only causing her anxiety to heighten. She twisted her hands together, noticing immediately the sweat that was forming on her palms. As she wiped her hands on her sides, she felt her legs tremble. "Umm," she started, glancing back at her mother and father. "I won't be choosing a king today. Thank you."

The crowd simultaneously gasped as hushed whispers spread like wildfire through the crowd of goblins. Strelitzia rushed off the stage and out of the great hall. She carried her long skirt, so she didn't trip on it while making her escape. As Strelitzia made her mad dash out of the room, her heart pounded, and her breathing was shallow. She dreaded what was to come from her mother and father.

Once Strelitzia had gotten herself out of the room, she slammed the stone door shut behind her, resting her back on its cool surface. She tried to steady her breathing, but all she could hear were the shouts of her settlement from the other side of the door.

"What does she mean she isn't choosing a king?"

"What does this mean for the Lýsa Crystal's illumination?"

"Are we all going to die?"

"Are we going to lose our gifts?"

"You need to force her!"

Strelitzia worried about the lecture that she was sure to endure from her parents. They had this talk, and she had told them that she'd have a decision made for today. With inner turmoil wreaking havoc, she just couldn't. This wasn't what she wanted. She froze as she heard her mother's voice above all the shouting goblins.

"Good goblins, please rest assured, our daughter will choose a king before the end of her seventeenth year. She is only in her early seventeenth year; she still has time. Please, do not fret. Everything will be okay." Queen Moonglade spoke with purpose, her calming voice booming through the room.

As calming as Queen Moonglade was, her voice carried an authority along with it that sent a chill down Strelitzia's spine. She had seen her mother be stern before. She had been on the brunt end of her sternness and had never liked how it made her feel. She knew her parents would be coming for her, and she dreaded what her father would have to say. He'd want to discuss her grand announcement, or lack thereof. She didn't know how else to explain to her parents that this wasn't the life she wanted. At least, not right now. This enormous weight of responsibility that was generationally placed on a seventeen-year-old only made her anxious and angry. Above all, though, through her anger, sadness, and annoyance, her heart ached most knowing she had disappointed them. All of them.

Chapter Two

Talking Potion

"I don't want to marry, not right now! I want to see the world!" Strelitzia, the emerald-green-skinned, purple-haired, and amethyst-eyed goblin, yelled to her parents as they continued to pester her about finding a suitable mate. Her large, pointed ears were slicked back like an angry cat. Tension ran at an all-time high every time this conversation was had. Strelitzia was ready to be Queen, academically. She knew the rules, the protocols, how to be proper and present herself as a Queen, but she wasn't ready for it emotionally. She felt she hadn't lived enough to be buried under mountains of responsibility.

"There are duties required in your position. Duties that need to be fulfilled. You are seventeen. You have only a short time, less than one final year to wed, or we risk the Lýsa Crystal's illumination extinguishing. Taking all our gifts along with it. We've talked about this relentlessly." King Verdant fired back at his daughter.

His voice was deep and harsh. Strelitzia was sure that her father had had enough of her antics and wanted her to understand the severity of her decisions. Which she did. She knew the weight of her decision, yet her heart still wanted her to make it. Strelitzia toyed with her mixture of fear, guilt, and desire. Fear of her father's wrath. Guilt of the potential gifts she could single-handedly take away from her people. And a strong desire to explore.

While Strelitzia stood, watching her father, with his stoic, perfect posture and his arms crossed, anger fumed from his oversized, sharp ears. She realized just how much he had changed over the years. His once equally emerald skin to hers had begun to fade into a green barely more vibrant than moss. His deep chestnut hair was rapidly thinning and losing its color, and his amethyst eyes were growing dim. Not nearly as vibrant as they'd once been. The stick and clover crown, glittered with gold dust, that sat on his head now seemed too big, since his hair had lost so much of its luster. At almost sixty, he was starting to become one with the earth. At that moment, Strelitzia realized her time with her father might be limited.

"I didn't ask to be a stupid princess. I should not be punished and pressured into doing something that I never signed up for! If you want a perfect heir, have another child." Strelitzia bit back, instantly regretting her words. She loved her life, enjoyed being a princess, and adored her settlement. She was fundamentally ready to be Queen. She knew she could handle it.

The rebellious teenage spirit, though, lived strongly inside Strelitzia. Her free spirit often took over her logical thinking. Typically, she had a level head and made good decisions. This topic, however, proved to be a difficult one with her. Her parents raised her to be proper and with a deep love of the goblin ways. As time went on and Strelitzia read, she discovered that there was more to the world than their mountain range, and she longed to see it all. In her mind, seeing and learning the other realms of Lurin would be greatly beneficial in her queenhood.

"Darling, we understand your desires, and you have your whole life to fulfill your dreams, but right now, you have a duty to your people. If you marry now, have a child right away, then you only have a short eighteen years before you relinquish your title and are free to do whatever your heart desires." Queen Moonglade said in a calm, soothing voice as she reached out and held her daughter's shoulder, smiling gently at her.

Strelitzia knew this was just a mother trying to soothe her daughter's anger, but it wasn't working. Her mother's deep juniper skin still somehow managed to shine, even though she was in her fifties, a time in a goblin's life when their transformation to the earth typically began, and their vibrancy began to fade. Her long plum colored hair was still full of volume, and her fuchsia eyes still gleamed in the moonlight. She stood tall with her flowered crown resting on top of her luxurious locks.

"Eighteen *short* years? Eighteen is a huge chunk of a goblin's life! That would only leave me ten-ish years before I'd start to become one with the earth!" Strelitzia nearly cried to her mother. Begging her to see reason, to understand her.

The Lumiara Mountains were a wondrous place full of lush, deep green grass, clover, and moss, and the tallest trees that swayed in the gentle breezes that passed them by. The mountains were hundreds of miles high and a light, glistening gray. They almost looked silver. There was a single stream that flowed through their home, starting at the top of the highest mountain, coming directly from the cavern which held the Lýsa Crystal, flowing down to the lake at the base of the mountains. The goblins had used the running stream for fresh drinking water and to prepare baths in their stone bathtubs, not that they bathed often. Goblins were rather dirty creatures. Every so often, a fish or two would find itself swimming down that stream, only to be caught and eaten. Each goblin mother and daughter had planted gardens outside their homes that were nestled deep into the mountainside with little light. Somehow, the flowers always grew, leaving vibrant colors littering their community.

Each home in Lumiara was carved intricately into the mountainside. They were all relatively small, maybe a single bedroom, one and a half if you were lucky. An alcove for using the restroom and a natural shower head to bathe. They had a community bathroom, which was home to four stone bathtubs. Each cave was dark and damp, with only the light of a fire to illuminate the main room. Because of this, the goblins developed incredible night vision. Then there was the royal home, the home that each royal family had lived in. Carved into the highest possible point of the mountain sat the largest cave. A four-bedroom, two-washroom home.

When the sun shone down on Lumiara, everything glistened with sparkling gold. The goblins used their brute strength to grind down anything gold they had recovered and sprinkled the dust around their homes. The goblins had a fierce craving for anything gold, shiny, and valuable; many of them would hoard gems and other trinkets they'd find while out hunting for food. They cared for their material things more than they cared for their loved ones. The Lýsa Crystal, though, was the prized possession of the goblins, which had never been moved from its original resting place. Within the royal home, down a long, dark hallway, and into a large cavern, sat the Lýsa Crystal, surrounded by offerings of gold, silver, and gems. The source of the goblin's magic. Their superhuman speed, their ability to never tire, their unwavering agility, their power to heal, their savage strength, and above all, their greatest joy, becoming one with the earth. No one goblin contained all the forms of magic, except for one: Princess Strelitzia.

When Princess Strelitzia formally announced her desire not to marry and to explore the world, all the goblins in Lumiara panicked. As far as Strelitzia knew from her studies, the Lýsa Crystal remained illuminated and radiated magic so long as a king and a queen were married and ruled over Lumiara. When a prince or princess was born, he or she had until the age of eighteen to find his or her other half and marry before the parents stepped down from their royal titles and passed them on to the next king and queen. With only one year remaining for Princess Strelitzia, the goblins grew tense. If they had no power, how could they protect themselves? However, according to Princess Strelitzia, since this had never actually happened, how could they be so sure? How could any of those goblins actually know that the Lýsa Crystal's illumination would die out if she didn't marry? None of them knew the status of the crystal before the goblins had discovered it.

Shortly after the continuous argument with Strelitzia's parents, she stormed off. Once inside her own room, she slammed the makeshift door made from tree bark and stone, making the mountain walls shake, and threw herself on her bed with a loud groan. She screamed into her pillow until her lungs hurt. She hated being told what to do. She hated being a princess even more. Crocus, a miniature dragon-fly, landed with a plop on Strelitzia's back and waddled his way to her head. He was not the most graceful dragon-fly. Once there, he blew a small smoke ring into her face.

"Crocus, not now." She said angrily to the tiny dragon-fly, without removing her face from her pillow, who, in return, blew fire at her, charring her long purple hair.

"Hey!" she yelled as she sat up and attempted to extinguish the flame. "What was that for?" The tiny dragon merely smiled, tail and butt wagging, like he was ready to play.

"Crocus, I'm not in the mood to play right now. They don't understand. My parents don't understand. You're lucky, you get to come and go as you please. You don't have rules to follow and an *image* to maintain." Strelitzia sobbed to Crocus. "I don't want to be queen right now. I don't want the royal responsibilities yet. I just want to explore. I want to go see where the vampires live and where the sirens dwell. Where the dragons roam and where the werewolves hide. I want to listen to the ocean and smell the salty air. I want to see what shops are in which towns. I want to go hiking in woods that aren't my own. I don't want to be tied down to Lumiara." The waterworks burst wide open, sending Crocus nearly floating down a river of tears. "Ugh, I'm sorry. I know you can't fly with wet wings. Let me help you."

Strelitzia gently lifted the dragon-fly, which fit comfortably in her hand, and heavily blew on his wings, sending all the water away, leaving his wings dry as a bone. Crocus eyed her and tilted his head before flying over to her locked cabinet that sat in a rounded corner of her room. He gently pawed at the doors before Strelitzia got the hint.

"Okay, okay, I'm coming." She said to him as she got up and walked across the cool dirt floor to her cabinet. She opened it and started pulling bottle after bottle from its shelves, reading each label carefully.

"You must love that I read so much and was able to concoct this potion." A hint of a smile finally danced on her lips.

"Found it." She held up a vial full of an electric green liquid. She swirled it around and watched as the evergreen shifted and mixed with swirls of lime green. She yanked the cork out of the top, and a small cloud of green smoke puffed its way out. The little dragon-fly quickly rushed to her hand, holding the bottle, and shoved its tiny nose into the opening.

"Easy killer." She laughed. When Crocus finally came up for air, he started rambling.

"Yes, I'm rather glad you were able to make this. I love having the ability to talk. It's really great. Do you love being able to talk? Because I *love* it when I'm able to talk. It's easily one of my favorite things to do. Wouldn't you agree?" The one thing Strelitzia hated most when Crocus would take this potion was that for the first thirty seconds, sometimes longer, the tiny pest wouldn't shut up, and he spoke so fast that she almost couldn't keep up.

"Are you done? Did you get it out of your system?" Crocus' voice was as tiny as he was. He almost sounded like a toddler, but with a much larger vocabulary.

"Umm, I think so. I'm not entirely sure, though. I'll let you know in a minute or two. Or maybe I have calmed, and I just haven't realized it because I'm just so excited! I have an idea for you, and I've been dying to tell you all about it, but you haven't been here, you've been gone, but now you're back, and I can finally tell you!" Crocus did little loop-the-loops in the air, full of excitement and happiness. Strelitzia envied that happiness, that carefree attitude; she wanted a taste of it for herself.

"Okay, you've got to calm down. Why don't you take a second to breathe?" Crocus nodded and flew his way back over to her bed, where he landed, not so gracefully, and started deep breathing exercises.

"Good. Now, what is your idea?" Strelitzia asked the little dragon.

"We should go see Master Gibbous!" He squealed as small sparks escaped his nose.

Chapter Three

Master Gibbous

Once Crocus had finally had a chance to calm down, the pair went to see Master Gibbous. Gibbous had been around longer than any goblin and was able to see things that had yet to happen. He still resided peacefully in his large redwood tree by the entrance gate of Lumiara; however, no one spoke of visiting him, at least not anymore. It was written in the history books that he had earned his peace and solidarity, and he should not be disturbed. Strelitzia, remembering what she'd read, started to wonder if this was such a good idea. Would the crystal be cross with her for disturbing him? Would Maker? She twisted her mouth as her brain played out possible scenarios.

"So, Strelitzia, what exactly does it mean to *become one with the earth*?" Crocus asked, breaking Strelitzia's train of thought.

"Well, once a goblin reaches its fiftieth year, it starts its transition to being one with the earth. The first Goblin to ever have this happen was Master Gibbous. Goblins have been under the impression that it was the Lýsa Crystal's doing. In this transition, the Earth prepares you. The goblin picks its dream location, a location where it will remain until the end of time. You then have thirty years to finalize your affairs before you fully become one with nature. Once you're done, you make your way to the spot of your choosing, and the earth eases you in. The roots of the tree wrap around your feet and ankles, and the bark of the tree accepts you in, until you are fully a part of the tree, with only your face visible. I've heard that it isn't a long process, it takes about an hour, and it's painless. Typically, Goblins choose trees; however, occasionally, a goblin chooses a more uncommon area, like the side of the mountain or within a flower bed. Gibbous chose the largest tree, at the entrance of the settlement, with the thought that from there, he could look after every goblin after him." Crocus nodded with what Strelitzia thought was understanding, but she really couldn't be sure.

"How does he talk?" Crocus questioned.

"That's what no one could see coming. The Maker chose Master Gibbous to stay. To become one with the earth but remain present, mentally and spiritually, to guide further generations of goblins. His insight into the future, predictions, and warnings have all come true in one way or another. He is a vital lifeline for the goblins. It really was a magnificent gift for him to be allowed to remain present while also being one with the earth." Strelitzia said as Crocus smiled and laughed.

"Well," he started. "It's a nice thought. I'll believe it when I see it."

The two continued in silence, allowing Strelitzia to return to her paranoia of disturbing Master Gibbous' peace.

After a while, they got to the entrance of the settlement. Strelitzia stared in wonder at the large entrance gate made of stems adorned with thorns, held up by two large tree stumps. With no wall on either side, which Strelitzia had always thought to be odd, anyone could simply walk around the gate. Resting just behind it was master Gibbous' tree. Strelitzia approached the tree cautiously, staring deeply into the closed eyes of Master Gibbous.

"Master Gibbous, I seek advice." Princess Strelitzia reverently kneeled in front of the large tree, placing a stargazer lily at its roots.

She had read that when you go to visit Master Gibbous, you must present a lily to him to honor his late wife. If you did not present a lily, he would not speak to you. She gazed into the face of Gibbous, his eyes still closed, with a smile on his lips. His long, flowing white beard and mustache cascaded down the tree, forming a pool of white at the tree's roots. Slowly, his eyes peeled open, and he let out a yawn. Strelitzia's eyes grew wide as she stumbled backward, tripping and falling over a root. She didn't fully believe that he was still *alive* within his tree. She had hoped so but didn't think it was actually true. Not all these years later. No other goblin had ever continued living once their transition to the earth was complete.

Strelitzia shrieked as she fell, landing with a hard thud.

"Aww, Princess, what a pleasure it is to speak with you. I've been expecting you, you know." Strelitzia remained on the ground, eyes still wide, and her mouth gaped wide open. "What advice do you seek?" His voice was shaky, which made it a little difficult to understand his words. She wondered if he had always sounded like this, or if his voice was the outcome of having been around for over one hundred years.

"Uh, hello, Master Gibbous. Thank you for speaking with me." Strelitzia said as she regained her composure and brought herself to her feet.

She felt a little silly speaking to a tree, but she continued anyway. "I wish to explore. If I, hypothetically, were to leave and not marry before I turned eighteen, what would happen to the Lýsa Crystal and its gifts?" Strelitzia held her breath and her hands, waiting impatiently for Gibbous's response.

"The Maker keeps silence where the Lýsa Crystal is concerned. Magic is not a language the Maker chooses to speak, nor a path the Maker walks. Though the goblins were brought into being by the Maker's design, the Crystal answers to no such origin. I fear, young princess, that wisdom sometimes offers only the truth of not knowing." Strelitzia slumped her shoulders as her head fell to Master Gibbous's answer.

She felt defeated. She had read that the Lýsa Crystal spoke to Mast Gibbous. Was that all a lie?

"However," Gibbous continued, spiking Strelitzia's interest. A sense of hope filled her heart. "At seventeen, your path has not yet narrowed. The year before your binding remains unwritten. A brush with the unknown may temper you more than sheltered time ever could. Yet know this, within these woods and across the realms beyond, there are eyes that see you not as a princess, but as a prize. What you do with this knowledge is yours to decide." Those last few words sent chills running up and down Strelitzia's spine.

"Please forgive me if this is a rude question, but if The Maker doesn't speak to you about the Lýsa Crystal, then how do you know so much about it?" A warm smile spread across the old goblin's face.

"It was I who uncovered it, in an age when I ruled. I protected it, listened to it, and taught its language to the goblins. The Lýsa Crystal spoke to me a single time, at our first meeting, and never again. Yet that moment endures. I believe it is the Crystal that anchors my soul to this world, not the Maker. For the Maker does not preserve, he recalls."

"Can you tell me about the smaller, colored crystals? I've heard stories, but I'm not sure how much I actually believe them." Strelitzia hoped she hadn't overstayed her welcome with this question, and a small amount of fear that he wouldn't answer crept into her heart.

"You are full of questions, aren't you? My dear girl, I recognize that hunger. I once carried it myself. The smaller crystals are the vessels through which the Lýsa Crystal shares its power with you. White carries raw energy. Purple grants sight beyond sight. Aquamarine mends what is broken. Starry black lends strength to those who can bear it. And on the rarest of paths, green, the power to bend the earth itself to your will. Should you ever find such a stone, guard it as you would your own breath. The old stories do not lie. The Lýsa Crystal does not hoard its magic; it pours itself into these fragments, threading its will so that its gifts may walk beside you, and quietly shape the lives you lead." Strelitzia stood shocked by Master Gibbous's words.

The goblins learned about the different colored crystals, but they didn't know that the Lýsa Crystal fueled them to work. This was the proof she needed. Answers from the one who knows the Lýsa Crystal best. Adrenaline and excitement flooded Strelitzia.

Master Gibbous's eyes closed again. Strelitzia slowly approached the tree, gently tapping on its bark. "Master Gibbous?" Nothing. Strelitzia assumed that meant he was done talking.

She had always thought he was just named after King Gibbous; there was, of course, speculation, but no one knew for sure that he *was* him. Strelitzia now knew with certainty. She rested her hand on the bark of the tree and silently vowed to keep his secret. She feared the masses that would crowd his tree, disturbing his eternal peace, if it ever came out that he still gave out advice.

"Thank you." She whispered.

She rose and started walking around the settlement with Crocus, once again, perched on her shoulder. Today, there was a cool breeze sweeping through the settlement. Spreading the fragrance of all the plants through the air. The gardenias and Freesias overpowered all the other flowers. The mix of grass and clover on the ground was soft and cushioned her chubby bare feet as she walked. She enjoyed spending time within the settlement, watching the children play, the mothers and daughters tending to their gardens together, the fathers and sons training to hunt and fish; it was all fundamental things that she wished she could do. Live an uncomplicated life. A life without demands and responsibilities. She longed for simplicity.

"Princess!" a small voice shrieked as she continued her peaceful walk.

When Strelitzia turned, she saw a small goblin chasing after her, waving a hand through the air. She smiled. Little Rosebud.

"Hello, how are you? How is school going?" Strelitzia knelt to be eye level with the young goblin.

"It's good, I guess. It's school." Rosebud said. Strelitzia laughed. She remembered her young education well, and it was, in fact, rather boring.

"What are you currently studying?" The little goblin put a finger to her chin, most likely for dramatic effect.

While she thought, Strelitzia really looked at her. She was dirty, sure, but her hair shone. It was two-toned, purple and blue, the only goblin to have such hair. Strelitzia figured she got made fun of for it, but she thought it was beautiful. Today, Rosebud had her hair in braids, three of them, the purple and blue fighting over which would be the center of attention. The little goblin had piercing green eyes and ears that Strelitzia hoped she'd grow into one day.

"We are learning about the old way. The discovery of the Lýsa Crystal and what it does. Oh, and gardening." Rosebud finally answered.

"Ahh, very important topics. I hope you're paying close attention. Some of that will be able to help you significantly as you grow." Rosebud smiled and hugged Strelitzia before running off to continue helping her mother.

Strelitzia knew she would miss being here while she was gone on her adventure, but she was determined to leave, nonetheless. She wanted to explore; it was the only thing her heart truly desired. She had come up with a plan and was going to see it through by any means necessary.

She turned a corner, around a large tree, and collided with Oleander. A strong, male warrior who was similar in age to her, only a few months older. They had been friends in school but were forced to go their separate ways. After their primary schooling was complete, Strelitzia went on with her royal studies, while Oleander started warrior training. Additionally, Strelitzia spent most of her time high in the tallest mountain that she called home. Oleander, being of a lower class, remained closer to ground level.

"Oof!" She exclaimed as she practically bounced off of him, and stumbled backwards, tripping on a root before she fell to the ground. How unprincess-like.

"Princess Strelitzia, I'm so sorry! I didn't see you coming." Oleander apologized as he reached down and lifted her with ease. Strelitzia didn't think she was an overly heavy goblin, but something about how he casually lifted her from the ground made her heart flutter.

"It's okay, I'm fine." She looked into Oleander's eyes and smiled. He had beautiful blue eyes. One of the only goblins to have them. They looked like the ocean and sparkled in the rare rays of the sun. She'd always loved his eyes.

As she admired him, an idea flashed before her. "Oleander, can you keep a secret?" She grabbed his hands and pulled him in close to her. The smell of the forest mixed with sweat radiated off of him.

She knew he could, and he would keep her secret. They'd kept each other's secrets for ages. Strelitzia knew that he had a crush on her, even though they were from different social levels, and knew they could never be together. He still pined for her, and if Strelitzia was being honest, she liked him too. Because of this, she knew he'd keep her secret, preparing for any opportunity to be with her. She had often dreamed of being with Oleander when they were younger goblins. Back before her father made it clear that her *mate* must be of one of the higher classes, shooting those dreams dead. Deep down, though, she remained hopeful. Oleander was one of the most attractive goblins she'd ever met. He was very tall and full of muscle, the type any warrior should be. He had shaggy but short blue hair, and his smile dazzled, showing off his sharp white teeth. His moss green skin, large, pointed ears, and ocean blue eyes were just bonuses.

"Of course I can." He laughed. "I heard about what happened. Are you okay?" Oleander seemed to be holding his breath while waiting for Strelitzia's response.

"I'd rather not talk about that," Strelitzia stressed.

She didn't want to relive the whole naming her husband ceremony. Oleander let out a sigh, smiled, and nodded, "How would you feel about going on an adventure with me?" Strelitzia moved on from the topic quickly.

"Anytime! What kind of adventure do you have in mind? Hiking a tough trail? Going hunting deep in the woods?" He sounded excited about the idea, which gave Strelitzia hope that he'd agree to go with her. Not that any of his suggestions were what she had in mind.

In their current ages, they didn't have a whole lot of responsibilities. Oleander was essentially on hold until a war broke out. He spent his time hunting with his father, or helping his mother around the house, while also attending routine training upkeep once or twice a week. Strelitzia spent her time reading. Studying up on the goblins in depth, taking etiquette courses, and perfecting her royal duties list.

"I want to explore. Specifically, Thornveil Isle." He paused and stood a little straighter. His smile slowly faded from his face, as did his coloring. His smile was replaced with a look of concern.

"The vampires? Why on earth would you want to go there? I'm pretty sure they hate us." Oleander said with genuine concern.

"We don't actually *know* that, though. What if they don't? We will never know if we don't go find out. What I do know is that I need to do it now, before I turn eighteen, and I think it would be smart for me to have a strong warrior with me to help me stay safe. They have an elixir that sounds amazing, and I really want to get my hands on it." Strelitzia could tell by the look on his face that Oleander was heavily debating this.

She could see the internal battle that was playing out in his head and hoped that his feelings for her would win the argument. She watched intently as his facial expressions changed, signaling each feeling. Nerves, annoyance, anger, acceptance, all written across his handsome face. She wanted to reach out and touch it.

"Strelitzia, I don't know. Sure, the vampires might not care about us, but they also might. What if we don't come back? What's so great about this stuff?" Strelitzia knew that he needed more answers before he agreed to this.

"We will come back. I have no doubts. The venom is sparkly, and it's said to help any potion's effects last longer. If I could give that gift to Crocus, I'd be the happiest goblin in

Lumiara." Strelitzia could tell that Oleander felt nervous about this whole idea and wondered what he was thinking. He had let go of her hands, which caused her heart to ache, and took a step back. "Care to share your thoughts so far?"

"How much trouble will I get in for assisting you on this journey? We'd obviously be discovered at some point once everyone realizes you're gone. This isn't a secret that would *stay* a secret. On the other side of that sword, could I potentially be honored for protecting you? For keeping you safe while you live out your dream?" Oleander rambled.

Of course. Strelitzia should've led with that. Why wouldn't Oleander be worried about the death penalty for escorting Strelitzia galivanting around the Realms of Lurin?

"I won't let that happen. Maybe my father will give you a shiny medal for keeping me safe. That seems like a much more likely outcome." Strelitzia hoped that the thought of a chunk of gold hanging around his neck was enticing. "We would get to spend time together as we used to when we were adolescents. I know I always enjoyed that." Now, Strelitzia was tugging on his heart string. The strings she knew were reserved for her. Between the idea of gold and her love, she knew he'd be sold.

"Alright, when do we leave?" Oleander caved, and Strelitzia's smile spread across her face. She jumped up and wrapped her arms around his neck, hugging him. Strelitzia closed her eyes and really embraced the hug, feeling every muscle in his back and arms. His scent was masculine and intoxicating. The butterflies in her stomach refused to die down. She planted a quick kiss on his cheek.

"You're the best! I want to leave as soon as possible. I'm thinking two nights from now. We probably need to leave when everyone is asleep, or my father will try to stop us." He nodded.

The thought of her father, the King, sent a small amount of doubt running through her. The King would not be pleased if he learned about her plan. They would need to be extremely careful.

"What should I prepare for our journey?" Oleander questioned.

"Um, stuff to set up camp would be helpful. Maybe some of whatever you guys use for hunting, you know, knives and stuff. A canteen for water, if you have one. That should be good. I'll gather food and other provisions of that kind and grab a map. I know my father has one somewhere. We are also going to need something to keep us really warm, it's very snowy and cold in Thornveil Isle." Strelitzia held out a finger for each item she listed until she had all five fingers of her hand outstretched.

"Two days, camping equipment, my bow and some arrows, probably a knife of some form, and thick moss coats. I'll have it all ready. What about protection from the vampires?" Oleander raised another valid question.

"We have Crocus. I've read that dragon fire can kill a vampire. Hopefully, Crocus' flame is big enough to at least render them unconscious for a while. Long enough for us to get away."

"Good enough for me." Oleander seemed edgy about the vampires, but Strelitzia hoped that having Crocus around would help put him at ease.

Her smile didn't falter as she raced back to her home to start preparing for their journey.

On the way back, she took in everything around her. The aroma of fresh cut grass and flowers, the smell of water mixed with limestone sitting in buckets, and the calming scent of lavender. She could smell the evening meals being prepared in each home. Some were cooking whatever meat they'd managed to catch that day, some had enticing vegetables, while others had fresh bread. It was making her mouth water. The cool breeze helped push these scents throughout the settlement, making the whole place smell amazing.

Crocus sat on her shoulder, happy as can be, with his eyes closed and chin tilted to the sky. His little nose was going a mile a minute. Strelitzia knew there were too many scents for him to take in at once, and it would overload his senses.

"Everything smells delicious! I'm so hungry." His voice cracked, and Strelitzia knew her potion was wearing off. This was one of the reasons Strelitzia wanted to go see the vampires. She wanted Crocus to be able to talk all the time, not just for a few hours every day, and she really hoped their elixir was the missing piece to her potion. It's rumored that Vampire Venom can heal, bring back youthful skin, and rejuvenate. It is also said, though, that it can be mixed with other potions to help make them more potent, which is exactly what she wanted.

"We'll eat something when we get back."

The remainder of their walk was peaceful, and neither of them spoke. Strelitzia was listening intently to the wind make its way through the treetops, tossing the leaves. Through the windchimes that some goblins had made out of their most precious trinkets, a magical melody was made. She'd miss the Lumiara Mountains that she'd always called home, but she knew this was her calling. She was born to explore, like the first generations of goblins. Whether she'd make it back or not was beside the point. She knew in her heart that her parents would mourn her if something happened. They wouldn't have an heir to take their place. She didn't know what that would mean for her settlement, but she fully intended to come back. At least, she hoped that she would. Thoughts continued popping into her head about what would happen if she didn't make it back. As hard as she tried to push those thoughts away, her heart just wouldn't let them go.

Chapter Four

The Lineage

T wo days later, Strelitzia was ready. Excitement and anxiety filled her to her core. She had stashed dried meats, fruits, and vegetables, along with a couple of loaves of bread from lunches and dinners. Had secured fresh water and filled two canteens made from mountain goat skin. After, she carefully wrapped her vial that allowed Crocus to speak in a clean cloth before placing it in her sack. Then, she found a map of their land and the surrounding areas and had it rolled up, carefully packed away. Strelitzia was ready. She only needed one more thing.

Strelitzia and Crocus quietly made their way out of her room and down the dark hall that led to the Lýsa Crystal. It was more beautiful than she had remembered. A light blue glow weaved its way throughout the hallway. She watched the blue ripples dance across the walls, ceiling, and floor like it was a show just for her. It was enchanting. She followed the water slowly, carefully, so she didn't fall, all the way to the Lýsa Crystal. She glanced down at the water that she was about to step into and hoped that it was safe. It would be rather unfortunate for her to die now, before her adventure even began. As she took the first step, the Lýsa Crystal seemed to freeze. She continued walking, with Crocus still on her shoulder, until she met the dirt that the Lýsa Crystal rested on. As she kneeled on the soft dirt, with her feet still in the water, she lowered her head.

"Lýsa Crystal, I feel rather silly speaking to you since you don't speak to anyone, but I need your help. I am to go on a grand adventure, one that will fulfill my life's dream. I wish to take a piece of you with me, along with a small crystal of each color to sustain my gifts, maintain my power, and keep myself safe. In return, I promise to come home before my eighteenth year begins and marry a worthy goblin. Please grant me this favor." Nothing. She didn't know what she had been expecting, but she had hoped for something.

After a minute, she got up and stared at the Lýsa Crystal, "It was worth a shot," she said to Crocus, who cooed at her; the potion now fully worn off. As she turned to walk away, she heard the Lýsa Crystal begin to crack. A ping of fear ran through her. Did she just break the Lýsa Crystal? Was that even possible? When she turned back around, it was glowing so brightly that she had to shield her eyes. It was loud, and she feared it would wake her father. Suddenly, it got dark. Very, eerily dark. She couldn't see anything, but she could still hear and feel the rumbling of the crystal. Strelitzia felt the temperature dramatically drop before a faint glow came from the ground. She breathed out and saw her breath float away from her. When she looked down, she saw a small piece of the Lýsa Crystal lying at her feet. She looked up at the Lýsa Crystal, "Thank you," she said with a smile.

She hesitantly looked at the shard of the Lýsa Crystal, weighing her options, knowing that the Lýsa Crystal didn't like to be touched. Would she be injured if she retrieved this shard? She convinced herself that she wouldn't. The Lýsa Crystal wouldn't have presented her with this gift if it meant to harm her, would it? She held her breath before reaching down and picking up the broken shard. She examined it in her hand, waiting for it to burn her palm. But it didn't. It felt smoother than it looked. As far as she knew, she was the only one to ever touch the Lýsa Crystal, or even a piece of it, and not be harmed.

Something else for your journey. A voice whispered through the air.

The ground shook violently. Strelitzia frantically looked around for something to help her steady herself. The dirt beneath the Lýsa Crystal began to part, pushing up a green crystal. Strelitzia's eyes grew wide, and a tingling started in her hands. It was beautiful and shiny. Strelitzia fought the greed that was building in her gut. Only one other green crystal had ever been seen. Had it been beneath the dirt all along? Are there more hiding down there? She pushed the thoughts away.

"For me?" She said with tears in her eyes, staring at the beautiful emerald in front of her. It was only a few inches long and a few inches wide, almost a perfect square, but it sparkled more than all the glitter in the settlement while in the large Lýsa Crystal's light.

For you. This crystal is powerful, but only when combined with me. Take the shard and the emerald and use them wisely. They will help you on your journey. I expect you will return it once your adventure has ended. These green crystals are precious and can be very dangerous if in the wrong hands. Gather small crystals of all colors for your journey and remain safe.

"Of course. Yes, of course!" She took both, thanked the Lýsa Crystal again, and left after she'd gathered the smallest of the other colored crystals she could find.

When she got to the large living room, the fire was nothing but smoldering embers, and the cave was silent. She looked around at the large stone couches that were draped in moss and jasmine, and the moss rug beneath her feet felt soft as she tiptoed over it. She was sad not to be telling her mother where she was off to and knew that she'd worry, but she couldn't risk her father finding out and preventing her from leaving. She debated leaving a note for her mother but immediately thought against it. She didn't want her father to find out her plans, and she couldn't risk her mother telling him. She let out a sigh as she put her hand on the door. As she turned around for one last look at her home, not knowing how long she'd be gone, she noticed a dark, shadowy figure at the end of the long hall, outside her parents' room. She froze.

The figure, locking eye contact, started to move forward. Strelitzia knew her plan was ruined. This was it. It was her father, and he was going to lock her in her room and throw away the key. Crocus made himself as small as possible, much like he did anytime he was ready to run and hide. She would be leaving Oleander in the woods, at night, by himself, and he'd have no idea what happened to her. Everything started to crash down around her. Her dream was ruined.

"My darling girl, take this with you." Queen Moonglade appeared with her arms extended towards her daughter, which signaled to Strelitzia that she wanted a hug. Strelitzia moved swiftly to her mother and melted into her embrace. "May my love keep you warm and protected."

"You're not mad?" Strelitzia asked her, a small sob escaping her throat.

"No. I know you must go and explore. It is in your blood. I also know that you would never let your settlement down. I have no fear that you will return to us before it's too late with a worthy goblin by your side." Her mother held her at arm's length before winking at her, placing a gentle kiss on her forehead, and making her way to the front door. Strelitzia wondered if her mother somehow knew that Oleander was going with her and if that was her subtle way of telling her that he was a worthy goblin. Another thought struck her as odd, though.

"What do you mean it's in my blood?"

"My darling girl, I believe it is time to tell you of your lineage. You are a direct descendant of King Gibbous and Queen Twilight. King Gibbous made a deal with the Lýsa Crystal to allow someone in his bloodline the ability to harvest all the powers of the crystals at once, as he had. This goblin would be able to speak to the Lýsa Crystal if it wished. The Lýsa Crystal asked in return that he remain here, mentally, for eternity. That special goblin is you."

Strelitzia's mind froze. Why her? What was so special about her?

"Now go, do not let questions or concerns plague your mind. You will need to have your wits about you for your journey. I am sure that Oleander will keep you safe. Be mindful of your surroundings. You never know when a surprise visitor will pop up. I will see you soon, my beloved." As Strelitzia opened the large front door, it made a slight creaking noise, and she shuddered. How does her mother know all of this? How did she know that Oleander was going with her?

Strelitzia didn't give her body time to process as she darted out of the door. She turned, one last time, towards her home and waved goodbye to her mother, who was standing in the shadows of their doorway. All she could see of her was the pearly white teeth in her smile and the glow of her dazzling fuchsia eyes.

As Strelitzia walked, she noticed just how dark it had gotten outside at night. Everything was calm, the canopy was still, no smells were wafting through the air, and it was pitch black. Crocus would spit fire every once in a while, in an attempt to light their way, but it never lasted long, and she didn't want to risk having him light a torch and waking any of the goblins.

Strelitzia could hear the night animals surrounding them. Owls hooted from far off, and the sound of bats soaring through the air, she thought she could even hear a dragon, a full-size one, on the hunt for food. It made her shiver. The ground beneath her feet was cold, not cool and refreshing, but cold. Freezing. She started to wonder if she should have brought something to cover their feet.

When they reached the meeting spot, Strelitzia sat down under a tree and waited. She didn't like waiting at night. She felt vulnerable. Like anyone could sneak up on her and attack. She reached into her sack and pulled out a knife.

Looking at it, she smiled. This knife had belonged to her grandmother, who had given it to her before she fully became one with the earth. *Here, my dear girl, this will keep you safe. Keep it close, never out of sight.* She could hear her grandmother's words in her mind, and it put her nervous system at ease.

Crocus squealed, bringing Strelitzia back to the now. She heard a twig snap, freezing both her and Crocus, eyes wide and ready for anything. As they waited, she could hear the sound of footsteps, crunching the dried leaves. Strelitzia gripped her knife as tightly as she could, ready to plunge it into someone or something's gut. Crocus reminded her of a cat ready to pounce. He had his butt in the air, his wings spread wide, and his fire building in his throat, ready to shoot.

"Strelitzia?" They both let out a sigh of relief. It was Oleander.

Strelitzia eased her grip on her knife and took a deep breath to steady herself.

"Hey." She responded, her voice shaky from the buildup of nerves releasing.

"You okay?" He appeared in front of her and instantly made her feel better. His size alone would scare off anyone in these dark woods.

"Yeah, just startled a little, that's all. Are you ready?" Strelitzia asked as a cold spell consumed her, making her entire body shiver.

"Yes," he tossed her a dark green, almost brown, moss cloak, which she threw around her shoulders and tied around her neck. Crocus nuzzled in close to the soft moss. "I brought these too. I figured if there's going to be snow, then we should probably cover our feet." Oleander smiled his infectious smile, causing Strelitzia to melt.

Strelitzia smiled in return, happy that he had thought of that, since she had not.

"This is perfect, thank you." She said as she pulled the cloak tightly around her.

For a moment, they were lost in each other's gaze. Unable to move. Crocus coughed, bringing them back, and the three took off down the mountain path as quietly as they could, with danger and the unknown echoing in each step.

Chapter Five

The Journey Begins

"So, what's our route?" Oleander asked Strelitzia after a horrifyingly silent few minutes. Listening to what the forest had to say was nerve-racking.

The low moans and growls of far-off creatures, the breeze disturbing the leaves of the trees, blended into an eerie crescendo. Add the sound of a twig snapping every few seconds, and the dried leaves crunching beneath their feet, and it was too much for Strelitzia's brain to remain on task, or her nervous system to remain calm. She wondered if Oleander felt the same, but assumed he didn't.

Oleander was an inculcated warrior for the goblin settlement. He was trained to fight, track, and be fully aware of his surroundings. She assumed that if they were in any danger, he'd know about it. He had never actually been to battle; there hadn't been one in decades, but he was prepared. He had graduated top of his class, earning him recognition from Strelitzia's father. He had broken every record set by those before him. His aim with a bow was near perfect every shot. His swordsmanship was unmatched. His ability to read tracks and find missing goblins or animals deep in the woods was top-notch. Strelitzia had always been amazed by Oleander and his skills. She couldn't imagine being able to do all the things he had accomplished. She had a special kind of pride for him.

"Well, I figure we need to go north. Through the forests of the fae to the water's edge. From there, we can figure out how to cross the waters to get to Thornveil Isle. We'll have plenty of time to figure that out; it will take us a couple of days, I suspect, to get to the waters." Strelitzia spoke as though she'd done this before, all while showing Oleander her plan on the map she'd packed.

"And what of the fae? How do they feel about us?" Oleander questioned.

Admittedly, Strelitzia didn't know the current state of their relations with the fae. Of course, there were stories, but how much could one really believe from a story that had been passed down from generation to generation? At some point, things became askew.

"I don't really know for sure what the current relationship with the fae is. I had read that we had a peaceful agreement with them during my schooling many, many moons ago. But all fae writing ended well before I was born. I have heard rumors that, recently, we established a truce with them, but I don't know all the details of it. As far as I know, we should be fine getting through their lands. We have our cloaks, and they should both hide our presence and our scent. I believe we can easily stay out of sight if we stick to the trees. They have primarily large redwoods, so it shouldn't be too difficult.

Besides, they live high above the ground in the treehouses." Strelitzia reasoned, and Oleander nodded his approval.

The trek through the mountainside in the middle of the night was treacherous. Strelitzia found herself tripping on exposed roots and fumbling her footing. Oleander always caught her, sending butterflies rushing through her stomach with each touch. She wasn't used to hiking on uneven surfaces, and it showed. But Strelitzia wanted to get to the fae border before they stopped. She wanted to be far enough away that her father wouldn't be able to send a team after her and drag her home. Luckily for her, Oleander not only knew how to track down lost goblins or beasts for the hunt, but he also knew how to cover their tracks. She watched in awe as he swished his extra-long cloak over their tracks, leaving them covered with dirt and untraceable.

"Are you okay?" Oleander questioned Strelitzia after another stumble over some pebbles in their path. He held her up and stared into her eyes with genuine concern.

"Yup, just fine, thank you," Strelitzia responded as chipper as she could.

"You keep tripping. Do you need a walking stick?" Strelitzia glared at Oleander. A walking stick? Like a cane that old goblins use? She wasn't that bad at this.

"How would that help? I'm tripping over roots." Strelitzia asked the question, genuinely confused by Oleander's suggestion. Oleander laughed in response.

"A walking stick helps you prepare for what's coming. You hold it out in front of you, and it will hit the roots before you get to them, so you don't trip." Strelitzia smiled and laughed nervously at the realization that a walking stick is not actually like a cane and felt silly.

"A walking stick would be lovely." She smiled at Oleander, then watched as he took off deep into the woods.

She didn't like being alone and unable to see him. She felt vulnerable. She wrapped her arms around herself and attempted to blend in with her surroundings. Oleander appeared moments later with a thick branch.

"Here." He said as he handed the large stick to Strelitzia.

"Thank you," She muttered in response.

After hours of walking, Strelitzia noticed the stars were starting to disappear. Neither had slept yet, and they'd need their rest. The Lýsa Crystal gave them incredible stamina, but even with the Lýsa Crystal's gift, they grew tired after too much strenuous activity.

"There's a cave up ahead. Do you want to stop? It'll feel like home." Oleander announced, as he jabbed Strelitzia's arm and smiled broadly. Strelitzia loved Oleander's smile. It was always genuine, never felt forced. She envied that. Being able to genuinely smile all the time sounded like something out of a fairytale.

"Sure," she said, "but no fire. I don't want anyone to know we're there."

Strelitzia was still worried about what her father might do once he realized she was gone. She feared the search party he might send that would drag her home, kicking and screaming. Worst of all, what he would do to Oleander for helping her. They were still technically in the Lumiara Mountains, still in his territory. She'd feel better once they got out of it. Once they cross the border, there will be nothing he can do.

Chapter Six

Surprise Visitor

Strelitzia woke up to birds chirping and sunlight pouring into the small cave they'd found, illuminating it entirely. She panicked as her heart started beating rapidly. She didn't want to be seen and was angry that the cave didn't provide the cover she had hoped for.

"Oleander!" She half yelled and half whispered as she bolted upright and hurried for the cave wall, startling Crocus in the process. She frantically looked around the cave, now well-lit by sunlight, but didn't see him. Which only caused her to panic more. Where was he?

"Crocus, where is Oleander?" Crocus shrugged and nuzzled back into a tiny ball, with his back to Strelitzia, and immediately started to snore. Strelitzia shook her head at the grumpy little dragon-fly. He has never been fond of being woken up.

Strelitzia took a few steps toward the cave opening, keeping herself as close to the cave wall as she could. When she peered outside, she saw him, and her nerves calmed. He was sitting in a ray of sunshine with his face aimed toward the sky. He seemed completely calm, but the daylight still made her nervous. The sight of Oleander, though, made her smile. She leaned her back against the wall and allowed herself to breathe normally for a few moments before she casually walked out and sat next to him.

"Good morning, Princess." He said joyfully as she plopped herself down next to him. Letting the morning light warm her face. She lay down in the tall, soft grass and let herself soak in all the nutrients from the sun's rays. Something that has always been a rare luxury back home. The sun rarely ever made an appearance beneath the massive canopy that covered the Lumiara Mountains.

"Don't call me that. You know better." Strelitzia smiled without looking over at him. He laughed, but even with her smile, she was serious. She sat up and looked directly into his dazzling blue eyes. "But really, I don't want the word *princess* thrown around on this adventure. I don't want anyone or anything knowing that I'm royalty. There's no telling what would happen to us." Oleander's smile turned quickly to a frown.

"Understood." That was all he said, but it was also all Strelitzia needed to hear.

They sat in the sun for only a few short minutes before they heard a branch snap close behind them. They both jolted their heads in the direction of the noise. Oleander pulled a knife out of seemingly nowhere, and Strelitzia was glad, all over again, that she had asked him to join her. His presence and quickness settled her anxious soul, and she was eternally grateful.

"What could it be?" Strelitzia asked Oleander as she hid behind him, peering around his large body.

"How should I know? I've never been this far from home." Oleander said without looking at her. Strelitzia watched as he kept a firm gaze in the direction of the noise.

"Will it kill us?" Strelitzia asked quietly. Oleander rolled his eyes and ignored her question.

"Come out now," Oleander yelled as he and Strelitzia stood. Prepared for anything.

After a moment, a nearby bush started to rustle, and a small goblin appeared out of it. Her face was monitoring the ground, and she held her hands behind her back.

"Rosebud?" Strelitzia questioned as she made her way from behind Oleander. "What are you doing here?" Strelitzia felt a wave of annoyance flood through her veins.

"I wanted to come with you. I couldn't sleep last night and saw you walking through the settlement outside my window. I got up and followed you because I was curious where you were going. Then I saw him and got even more curious. So I kept following, but then we got so far from the settlement that I didn't know how to get back home. I slept in that bush last night. It wasn't very comfortable." Strelitzia put her hand to her forehead and forced herself to calm down.

This is the surprise visitor her mother had warned her about. It had to be. She walked over to Rosebud and gently pulled small twigs and leaves from her hair.

"We have to take her back," Strelitzia said to Oleander. He nodded.

"No!" Rosebud yelled. "I want to go with you. If, when you were nine, and you had this chance to do something incredible, wouldn't you take it too? I don't know where you're going, but I want to come too!" This struck Strelitzia's heartstrings.

The little goblin was right. Strelitzia had wanted to explore since she was a young child. If she had been presented with the opportunity, she would've taken it also. She couldn't blame Rosebud for being curious and wanting to go on an adventure. She also couldn't find it in her heart to deny Rosebud the experience. If she did, then she'd be no better than her own father.

"Fine," Strelitzia said. "You can come. But you stay close. You do not wander off on your own, and you have to listen to everything Oleander and I tell you. Deal?"

Rosebud nodded her head furiously, "Deal. I promise!" She held out her pinky to Strelitzia, which made her smile.

She reached out with her own pinky, linked it with Rosebuds, and they shook on it. The pinky promise made Strelitzia remember her childhood and how common these had once been. A pinky promise was the equivalent of a signed, binding contract for the young. She couldn't even remember when she stopped making pinky promises but wondered if the return of pinky promises among the adult goblins could fix some issues with a little help from nostalgia.

"It's bad luck to break a pinky promise, you know." Strelitzia smiled at Rosebud.

"I don't plan on breaking it," Rosebud replied confidently.

They spent their time walking, eating, drinking, laughing, and taking in all that the Lumiara Mountains had to offer. The tall trees, the sounds of the birds and other small creatures that lived within the forests of the mountains, and the smells of flowers and fresh grass. Occasionally, they'd even experience cool breezes. Crocus's tiny claws began to dig into Strelitzia's shoulders like needles.

"What is it?" Strelitzia asked, feeling his tiny body stiffen. She reached into her pack and pulled out her potion to allow him to speak. He shoved his nose into the bottle, as he'd always done, and took a deep breath of the fumes.

"There's more of me. I mean my kind. They're nearby. I can smell them. I can hear them. They're here! Can you hear them? Can you sense them too? I can. I know it's more dragon-flies!" He paused to take a breath, return to his statuesque position, and listen. As did they all.

Suddenly, a swarm of tiny dragon-flies circled them. Hundreds of thousands of them in all colors flew around their heads and high above them. Making a spectacular show. Crocus jumped up and down joyfully before joining them in the air. Strelitzia looked over at Rosebud, enjoying the wander in her eyes as they watched the show, wondering if the little goblin would ever experience something like this again. Sure, others had dragon-flies within the goblin community, but not nearly this many lived among them, nor did they live with the lower class.

The three sat as Crocus got to play with the other dragon-flies. It brought joy to Strelitzia. She had always wondered if Crocus missed being with his kind; this was the proof she needed that he did. Sadness filled her heart at the thought of keeping him away from them. She sank into herself with guilt.

"Crocus?" She said softly. Crocus flew back down to her, out of breath, but with a big smile on his face.

"You look sad. Why are you sad?" Crocus asked her, and she forced a smile.

"Would you rather stay here with them?" Strelitzia asked the question and dreaded the answer. Crocus tilted his head, confusion written across his face.

"Why? Why would I want to leave you? You're my best friend." Crocus's confession made Strelitzia smile, but her guilt remained. Crocus grinned broadly before he pushed off and took to flight once again.

After a while, the dragon-flies flew off, leaving a rainbow of dust behind them. Strelitzia watched as Crocus landed on the ground and bid his kind farewell.

"That was fun," Crocus told Strelitzia. "Let's keep going."

The foursome stopped two more times to rest and let Rosebud sleep before they got to the edge of King Verdant's territory. Crocus was given small doses of Strelitzia's potion so he would be able to participate in conversations, but it never lasted longer than a couple of hours, and Strelitzia wanted to preserve what she had. She couldn't wait to mix it with the Vampire Venom and see if her idea would actually work. The thought of Crocus being able to speak to her for days at a time fueled her ambition.

"Um, I'm hungry," Rosebud announced as her stomach let out a loud rumble.

"I can hear that," Oleander laughed. "Let me go see if I can find something a little more nourishing than dried meat, fruit, and vegetables."

The bread Strelitzia had packed was long gone, now having a young goblin with them. She didn't want Rosebud to feel hungry or for any reason stunt her growth. If goblins didn't eat correctly and regularly as children, they wouldn't grow as tall. She wasn't worried about herself or Oleander. They were grown; they could stand to be hungry for a while.

Strelitzia, Rosebud, and Crocus found a quiet spot within the forest to sit and relax while Oleander went hunting. The rocky side of the mountain was a perfect spot to lean on and gaze into the wilderness of the forest. With Strelitzia's back against the rock and bottom on soft clover, she relaxed.

"We need to start looking for another stream, too. We're running low on water." Strelitzia announced to Rosebud, shaking the canteens she had packed, now almost empty.

They hadn't drunk an abundance of water, but they had already filled them once, and again, Strelitzia didn't want to deprive Rosebud. She had packed them, only expecting two goblins and a tiny dragon-fly to be drinking from them. Adding in Rosebud was taking its toll on their provisions.

"I can help," offered Rosebud. "I feel like I haven't been much help. I feel like I've just been taking and giving nothing back. Mother says that if you accept a gift or help, you should repay." Strelitzia could see something in Rosebud's eyes. Guilt? Sadness? She couldn't be sure.

"Your mother is wise, and I know you will when you are able. There hasn't been much yet that you've been able to assist with." Strelitzia put her arm around the young goblin and felt as Rosebud relaxed into her embrace.

Strelitzia was worried that this adventure would be too much for Rosebud and was second-guessing her decision to allow her to join them.

"How worried do you think your mother is about you?" Strelitzia asked. Rosebud stiffened, and her eyes grew wide.

"I hadn't thought about that," the young goblin admitted, "I just knew I wanted to go. Do you think she'll be very angry with me?" The look on Rosebud's face stabbed Strelitzia's heart.

"Maybe. I think she will be more worried than angry. We'll have to do something to make it up to her when we get back." Rosebud nodded, but didn't fully relax again, and Strelitzia immediately regretted saying anything. She hadn't spent a whole lot of time with younger goblins, but she should've known better.

What felt like hours later, Oleander returned. With him, he carried four small animals.

"Did you bring us clumps of moss to eat?" Rosebud asked, with a disgusted look on her face. Oleander laughed.

"No. These are Mosssprites. They're small rodent-like animals with moss-like fur that helps them hide from predators. They live near bodies of water mostly. Like lakes, rivers, waterfalls…"

"Water! If you found those, there has to be water nearby, and we need to fill our canteens." Strelitzia interrupted

Oleander, filled with a new excitement that replaced any thoughts of regret.

"Okay, we can do that but first let's get a fire going so we can cook these." Strelitzia watched Oleander set the small animals down and gather sticks from the surrounding area. Rosebud seemed overly eager to help him with this part.

After they had piled them into a small mound, he asked Crocus if he could assist with the flame. While Crocus got the fire started, Oleander used his knife to clean the Mosssprites. Strelitzia was intrigued by the process. She had never seen a goblin skin an animal before. She had studied it and the reasoning behind it, but seeing it firsthand? This was new. She watched as he sliced through their bellies and practically ripped their fur from their flesh. The sound made Strelitzia cringe and grit her teeth. This seemed barbaric.

He hung their fur on sticks and then shoved the sticks into the ground directly in front of the fire. He then shoved more sticks through the animals that he had cleared of any organs and handed one to Strelitzia, Crocus, and Rosebud. Strelitzia looked at the uncooked animal in front of her with slight disgust. Crocus, being an impatient little dragon-fly, torched the animal himself and devoured it whole before he curled up next to Strelitzia and took a nap. Strelitzia was amazed at how fast Crocus ate something that was nearly twice his size and started to wonder how much he could actually eat.

"What are you doing with their fur?" Rosebud asked as she watched the blood from the tiny creatures trickle its way down the hides and puddle on the ground.

"We do not take any part of nature for granted. These Mosssprites sacrificed their lives to ensure ours continue. We must treat all of them with respect and not be wasteful. Their skins will be used in other ways. Their innards and bones will be dispensed to fertilize the ground. We eat the meat and thank them for their sacrifice." Strelitzia explained to Rosebud.

When a goblin is in their adolescence, they learn to be very conscious of the earth and what it provides for them. It was instilled in all goblins that they do not own the earth and that goblins are not entitled to what the earth provides. That they borrow from it and never take more than they need, giving back to it as often as they can. Strelitzia, being royalty, had this imprinted in her mind. Lower-class goblins learn this, but it's minimal. It's a brief discussion over the course of a week of their schooling. Royals? It's a year-long affair. They learn in depth what the earth provides and the proper ways to honor the land's gifts. Strelitzia had been trained in these ways; she hadn't just learned them, as well as being taught the ability to educate others of the same.

"We can use them to make something to cover your feet," Oleander added. "If we are going to be dredging through snow, you'll need something. Four should be more than enough to make socks for your little feet." Rosebud giggled as Oleander tickled her toes.

Strelitzia smiled at the encounter, as warmth filled her heart.

"I feel like I'm in school," Rosebud said. Both Strelitzia and Oleander laughed.

"You asked." Oleander finally replied.

While the Mosssprites were cooking, Oleander took the two canteens and left to find water. By the time he returned, the Mosssprites were ready to eat, and their canteens were full again. The three sat around the small fire, enjoying its warmth and eating their meal, the first meal of fresh meat they'd had in two days.

"Will the smell attract other animals?" Rosebud asked, not taking her eyes off her food.

Strelitzia looked over at Oleander, now concerned by Rosebud's question, but Oleander didn't look phased. Strelitzia hadn't thought of that; she wondered if Oleander had. She began to scan their surroundings nervously. Expecting some giant beast to jump out of the tree line at any moment.

"Maybe." Oleander's voice pulled her from her paranoia, "However, I haven't seen any large animals around here, or even tracks, so I'm sure if it does attract anything, it will be something small. Which I can handle." Oleander responded before he took a big bite out of his mosssprite.

Strelitzia watched as juices oozed out of the animal and dripped down Oleander's chin before he wiped them away with his forearm. Watching this was odd and disgusting for Strelitzia. She couldn't hide the look of horror on her face. She had been raised to always use proper manners. Picking up and gnawing on your food was strictly against the rules of etiquette. However, they had no plates, silverware, or napkins, so what other choice did she have? She picked up her mosssprite daintily and took a small bite. It was delicious. She threw her training out the window, taking a larger bite.

When they were done eating, Strelitzia stood, held her hands out by her sides, and lifted her face to the sky.

"Maker," She started, and Oleander and Rosebud immediately stood up, assuming the same position as Strelitzia. "We thank you, and we thank the Mosssprites that were consumed today. May their remains provide nutrition for your earth. May their meat provide nutrients for our bodies and may their hides keep us warm." They all lowered their heads and held hands. Giving a moment of silence to the Mosssprites.

"Alright, let's get going. I want to find a cave to camp in for the night." Strelitzia announced as she nudged Crocus softly. Crocus growled in protest at being woken from his nap.

When he finally got up, the three goblins were staring at him expectantly. "Are you ready now?" Strelitzia asked him impatiently.

Chapter Seven

The Green Crystal

The border between the realm of the goblins and the realm of the fae was a magnificent one. Lined with tall redwood trees that stood at least twenty feet high and twenty feet around. On the goblin side, they were a more subdued red, while on the fae side, they were more vibrant. The trunks almost seemed to twist upward. Their tops created a broad canopy of gorgeous evergreen needles, which only let through small beams of sunlight. The sunlight would dance on the forest grounds, swaying when the wind would blow, sparkling.

"Wow," Rosebud said in pure amazement when she looked up at the massive trees.

"These are the redwoods. They are the biggest trees in the forest. There's nothing else like them," Strelitzia responded.

"They're pretty," Rosebud said as she gazed up to the tops of the redwoods.

"Do we know if it's safe to go through? Do the fae have any traps in place?" Oleander asked Strelitzia, who had no answer.

"I hadn't thought about that," she admitted. "I don't have the slightest clue. I'm not turning back, though, so I guess there's only one way to find out."

The four stood and weighed their options.

"Option one, we go through and find out there's a trap and find a way to deal with it. Option two…well, there is no option two. Only option one." Strelitzia told Oleander.

She hadn't thought to research the border; she just knew which way she wanted her adventure to go, and it was through the realm of the fae. Guilt consumed her thoughts of the unknown she was leading Oleander and Rosebud into. She could kick herself for not having researched this. These goblins were following her lead blindly, and she was possibly leading them straight into danger. Or worse. Death.

High above, Strelitzia heard the shrill scream of a raven.

"Well, that's not a great sign," Strelitzia said before placing her hand on her forehead.

"What was that?" Rosebud asked. Strelitzia pinched the bridge of her nose and squeezed her eyes shut. A raven was not what she wanted to hear.

"That was the cry of a raven. Ravens are said to bring messages from Maker, but also to warn of death." Oleander told Rosebud. Rosebud's eyes grew wide, and she swallowed hard.

"Death?" There was fear deep in Rosebud's eyes that accompanied her question.

"No one is going to die." Strelitzia took out the small vial and opened it. "Crocus, here," Strelitzia held the open vial out for Crocus, who greedily shoved his nose inside.

When he looked back up, he opened his mouth to talk, but Strelitzia pinched it shut with two fingers, cutting him off. "Would you be willing to fly through and see if you can spot any traps that might be waiting on the other side? I think you're small enough not to set anything off."

"I can do that. I would love to do that. I was going to suggest that. I'll be right back! Don't go anywhere. Don't leave me. I will be right back. RIGHT BACK!" Crocus flew away quickly.

While Crocus was gone, Strelitzia felt an electric shock from inside her pack that shot straight into her spine.

"Ahh!" She exclaimed before she dropped the pack to the ground.

"What's wrong?" Oleander asked, concern dripped from his words.

As she dug through her backpack, the weather began to shift. The sky was slowly covered by dark clouds, and a heavy wind began to pick up speed. The three looked around, confused.

"What in the world?" Oleander mumbled.

"I don't know," Strelitzia replied, as Rosebud grew closer to her, wrapping her arms around Strelitzia's waist. "It's okay, there's probably just a storm coming."

"If this is a storm, then we need to find shelter, fast," Oleander said to Strelitzia sternly.

"What about Crocus? I'm not leaving him!" Strelitzia then turned to the redwoods, cupped her hands around her mouth, and started yelling for Crocus to come back. There was urgency and panic in her voice as the storm continued getting worse.

As they waited, lightning struck the ground in front of them, leaving a charred hole in the earth. They all jumped back and stared first at the hole, then up to the sky. Strelitzia snatched up her pack and slung it over her shoulder. The leather was hot as it hit against her back.

"Ahh!" She screamed as she almost dropped it once more. She began furiously rifling through it. She grabbed a wad of fabric as more lightning struck a nearby tree, splitting it in two. She gently took the wad out of her bag and unwrapped it, making sure not to drop its contents.

"Is that a *green* crystal? Where did you get that?" Oleander took a few steps away from Strelitzia, pulling Rosebud with him and shoving her behind him.

The green crystal was glowing brightly next to the shard from the Lýsa Crystal. A visible stream moved from the shard to the emerald, powering it. Strelitzia was mesmerized by this action; she'd never seen it actually done before.

"The Lýsa Crystal gave it to me. Told me it could be helpful on our journey." Strelitzia said.

"Do you know how to use it?" Oleander looked at Strelitzia with worry on his face.

Strelitzia shook her head, "It didn't tell me that part. Let's try it, though."

Strelitzia tried to steady herself as she held the two crystals in her hand while rain started to beat down. The crystals burned and stung, and she could feel the power from the green crystal filling her veins. Strelitzia strained through the pain to remain holding the two crystals. Oleander continued taking slow steps backward, still shielding Rosebud. Strelitzia closed her eyes and tried her best to figure out what to do.

I want to move the trees out of my way. To create a clear path for us to get through the realm of the fae. Please help me. She thought to herself. Moments later, the earth began to rumble harder than any earthquake that had been felt in the Lumiara Mountains. Strelitzia, Oleander, and Rosebud struggled to stay on their feet as the ground shook viciously. Finally, everything stopped shaking, and the sky cleared, revealing the sun once more.

Two of the large redwoods slowly moved apart from each other. The deafening sound of roots ripping from the ground made Strelitzia shudder. She watched as the roots became almost like hundreds of little feet, moving the trees easily across the dirt and grass. As they moved, they left large crevices in the earth that quickly refilled and covered themselves back up. Once in place, the roots buried themselves back into the ground, and grass quickly regrew to cover the exposed dirt. Strelitzia stood shocked and amazed. She had done that with her mind. She glanced down at the jagged emerald in her hand and smiled.

They could see through into the realm of the fae; it was beautiful, but there was no sign of Crocus. The ground began to shake again, not as viciously this time, slowly forming a path of rubble and clover, lined with the most dazzling white daffodils Strelitzia had ever seen. The three stared in wonder as a perfect path was gracefully laid out before their eyes.

"Where does it lead?" Rosebud asked after everything had calmed. Still clinging to Oleander.

Strelitzia stared down at her hand holding the two crystals, which were no longer glowing. They hadn't burned her, and she wondered if Gibbous' blood coursing through her veins was to thank.

"I'm not sure, but I would assume it takes us straight through the realm of the fae. I believe we should trust the green crystal. I don't believe it would lead us astray." Strelitzia didn't look up from her hand, still in amazement at what these two small stones could do.

"Wow!" Rosebud exclaimed.

At that, Strelitzia finally looked up and over to Oleander and Rosebud, who were both smiling widely, in pure amazement. Seeing them not scared warmed Strelitzia's heart.

The Lýsa Crystal was right; putting this emerald into the wrong hands could be deadly. Strelitzia shivered at the thought of the damage that could be done with this small, green stone. She quickly wrapped the crystals back in their cloth and tucked them into her bag.

"How far is it to get through the realm of the fae?" Oleander asked, staring off down the newly paved path.

Strelitzia dug out her map, opened it up, and laid it on the ground. She could feel Oleander and Rosebud looking over her shoulder. Their breathing was rather distracting.

"About eight hundred miles, give or take a few, to get to the edge of the fae's realm." Rosebud's mouth dropped at Strelitzia's words.

"*Eight Hundred.* That's so many! How long is that going to take?"

"Well, if we keep a rate of about sixty miles a day, I'm going to guess that it will take us about thirteen days. We will then have to cross roughly four hundred miles of water to even get to Thornveil Isle. Not sure how we're going to do that. Then the capital of Heedmore, if this map is correct, is another five hundred miles inland. Then we get to make the whole trek back to the Lumiara Mountains. Making a round trip of approximately four thousand miles, or a little over two months. Plus, however long we have to linger on Thornveil Isle to get what we're looking for." Rosebud's mouth didn't close at Strelitzia's words. She was still in shock at how long this was going to take. Strelitzia looked at her expectantly for some sort of reply.

"That's so long!" Rosebud exclaimed. Oleander let out a quiet laugh as he sat back on the ground, pulling out his knife to sharpen.

"Rosebud, don't you think these were all questions you should've asked *before* announcing you wanted to come?" Oleander asked her, to which Rosebud didn't respond.

"Once we get to Thornveil Isle. We will have to navigate our way to Heedmore, the capital, to find the Vampire Venom from the Everthorne family. Then somehow convince a vampire to give us some." Strelitzia continued.

"Or steal some." Oleander chimed in while still sharpening his knife. Strelitzia gave him a chastising look.

"We are not going to *steal* anything. We will buy some." Strelitzia couldn't believe that Oleander had just suggested they steal something. She was royalty; stealing for her was instant death and potentially cause for war.

"Hello, company!" Crocus yelled as he plopped down on Strelitzia's shoulder. "I didn't see any traps of any kind, but the weather went a little mad, and then the trees all moved, and then a path appeared, but no traps. At least I didn't see any traps." Everyone let out a laugh at Crocus' expense. "Was it something I said?"

"Thank you, Crocus. We were just discussing the longevity of our adventure with little Rosebud. It seems she didn't realize how long we'd be traveling." Strelitzia quickly filled Crocus in.

"You brought a strength crystal with you, right? Once you cross the border, it won't work unless you have one on you. I hope you remembered the strength crystal with all the walking we're about to do. Did you?" Strelitzia was ready for the potion to settle, so Crocus would quit talking a mile a minute.

"I have one of each," Oleander announced, and Strelitzia took a deep breath.

"I do too," Strelitzia added, smiling at Oleander and his thought to be prepared. She stared at him a little longer than she probably should have. Really taking him in. She had always found him attractive, but something about him protecting them and remembering all the things that Strelitzia didn't made her body tingle and somehow made him more attractive to her.

Strelitzia refocused on the path ahead of them. A mix of nerves and excitement rushed through her. Just a few more steps and she'd be outside her father's territory. Outside his reach. The thought was rejuvenating but also terrifying. She'd no longer have his protection. A bit of doubt sparked within her as she thought about the dangers that she might face. She looked down at Rosebud, who was now holding her hand and looking up at her. How could she have been so careless as to let this young goblin join them? It was by far the most irresponsible thing she'd ever done. However, maybe if she had done this at her age, they wouldn't be here now, and her parents wouldn't be disappointed with her. She would've been ready to choose her husband.

"Are you ready?" Oleander asked her, breaking her from her thoughts. She nodded, and the four crossed over into the realm of the fae.

Chapter Eight

Encountering Fae

Nebraria was a beautiful place with near-perfect temperatures. It never got too hot, was always cool, and had refreshing breezes. At least that's what Strelitzia had read. Strelitzia had read that the fae live in elaborate treehouses, and she longed to see one. Having only lived in caves, Strelitzia was in awe at the thought. How ingenious to build a home high above the ground, away from dangers. Strelitzia looked out at the mile upon mile of land laid out before her and took a deep breath. The air here seemed cleaner than back home.

"Who are you? How did you make those redwoods move?" When Strelitzia turned, she was faced by three fae men. The three men all looked fairly similar. They had long, silvery, blond hair with a tall, slender frame with some muscle. Strelitzia had never seen this color of hair before, but she found it to be beautiful.

Strelitzia froze as she grabbed hold of Rosebud's arm and gently positioned her behind herself. She could feel Rosebud's small hands grip her forearm in return. How had Crocus missed them? Where did they come from? Had he even looked for actual fae, or was he too focused on finding traps?

"Good day, I don't fully know how we made them move if I'm being honest. I wished for them to move so we may pass, and then they did." Strelitzia replied almost honestly. Truthfully, she knew the green crystal did it, but she wasn't sure of how it actually all worked. She also refused to let on that she possessed a green crystal. She didn't know to what extent the other realms knew of the crystals.

The fae men seemed to stare into Strelitzia's soul. She felt uncomfortable and vulnerable. She nonchalantly nudged her bag further behind her back, hoping that the crystals within were not glowing. She didn't know if their light would be able to be seen through the thick hide of her bag.

"What are your intentions, goblin?" The fae standing slightly in front of the other two asked. Strelitzia believed he was the leader of this small group, since he was the only one speaking.

"We wish to travel through Nebraria to get to the ocean," Strelitzia said, as Oleander moved closer to her and Crocus sat comfortably on her shoulder.

"Why?" Strelitzia was confused; hadn't she already said why they wished to travel through their land? What was he looking for?

"We are just exploring the realms. We mean no harm. We're very intrigued by how other creatures live." What appeared to be the head of the fae men standing before them motioned to the others. It seemed to be some discrete form of communicating.

"I'll be blunt with you, goblins. Are you here for fae blood?" Strelitzia stood both shocked and confused. With one questioning eyebrow raised, she wondered why she should want fae blood?

"I'm sorry, but why would I want fae blood?" Strelitzia was genuinely confused, and it showed on her face.

Was this something that troubled the fae? Did creatures actually come here in hopes of gaining fae blood? What did they need it for?

The fae men glanced around at each other, each with an equally confused expression, much like her own. Strelitzia began to worry that this may be the end of their journey. If these fae didn't let them pass, she'd be forced to go home.

"Do you really not know?" Strelitzia glanced at Oleander, who simply shrugged his shoulders at her. "Fae blood is stolen often. For various reasons. You cannot pass if that is your intention. Do not lie, we will know." Strelitzia didn't understand. Why would anyone want to steal fae blood?

"I'm sorry, but I don't understand. Why would any creature want to steal your blood? I assure you, that is not why we're here." A cool breeze brushed past the group, giving Strelitzia a slight chill. She was mesmerized by their long hair gently flowing with the wind.

"If you don't know, then we'd rather keep it that way. We won't be the reason you learn others' heinous ways. What do you have to secure safe passage? There must also be something in this deal for us." Strelitzia wasn't sure what she had to offer. She had gold coins, but she doubted they'd want that. She assumed something as common as gold coins wouldn't grant them passage. She also had the crystals. The colored crystals.

"We have a few gold coins," This got an odd expression from the fae men that Strelitzia couldn't quite read, and she wondered if they didn't use gold coins, "or," she continued, "I carry with me a couple of the magic crystals from Lumiara. I have white, which emphasizes energy. I also have aquamarine, which promotes speedy healing. Finally, I have purple, which increases agility. Would any of these satisfy you?" Strelitzia stood tall.

She didn't feel fear, per se, but she was nervous. She needed these fae men to let them pass. The fae men glanced around at each other, whispering something she couldn't quite make out. As they awaited the fae's response, Strelitzia took a moment to glance down at Rosebud, who still clung to her arm. Rosebud's small face looked scared, and it ripped at her heart.

"You have white crystals in your possession?" The head male asked Strelitzia, full of intrigue.

"Yes, but just one." Strelitzia kept her lie brief. The fae men discussed amongst themselves again before returning their attention to Strelitzia's group.

"A white crystal will do nicely. Hand it over, and you may proceed. But do not stray from your path; we will be watching you. You won't see us but believe me when I say that we are there." Strelitzia gulped at the sternness in his voice.

The fae male put his hand out, and Strelitzia noticed how thin it was compared to her own chubby one. She glanced down at her hand, briefly wondering if being thin was attractive to the fae. If that were the case, were these men repulsed by Strelitzia and her group for not being slender?

Strelitzia took her bag off her shoulder and began to sift through it. She found the one white crystal she had and was glad that Oleander had thought to bring one as well. If she had to give up this crystal for them to continue on their journey, with the permission of the fae, she'd do it. She slowly held out the crystal in her hand and watched as the lead fae male gently took it from her. He examined it in the sun and smiled as it gracefully reflected the sunlight. He finally looked back and nodded to Strelitzia before the group of fae turned and walked away. Leaving Strelitzia feeling slightly unnerved by the thought of being constantly watched and the fae possessing a white crystal.

Strelitzia looked over at Oleander, who appeared to be as lost and confused by the encounter as she was. His head was slightly tilted, and his eyebrows furrowed. What did creatures want with fae blood? She shook the thought and focused on their journey.

Strelitzia felt a sense of relief being in Nebraria and out of her father's reach. She felt she could breathe easier, and she felt lighter, like a weight had been lifted off her shoulders. She smiled as they walked. She took deep breaths of the cool, crisp air, filling her lungs. Took in the scents of the redwoods and the feel of the soft moss. It was odd to her that the moss here felt different than the moss back home, and she wondered why. It felt softer, fluffier even, and was a more vibrant green. She watched as small bugs fluttered their way past them and loved how Crocus would playfully chase after them.

The ground beneath them was a dirt path, sprinkled with small pebbles that shone in the sunlight. The white daffodils that lined the road sounded like they were singing in the wind and appeared to be dancing. Was that possible? Was this an added little bonus from the green crystal? The tall redwoods loomed over their path, casting shadows of shade, giving the group relief from the rays of the sun that they weren't used to. Although Strelitzia was grateful for the shade, she thoroughly enjoyed the warmth that the sun provided her.

"It's so pretty here," Rosebud announced, breaking Strelitzia's train of thought.

"It really is. It feels so pure. Peaceful." Strelitzia added.

"The trees are so big, and they're everywhere. Look at that one! There's a house in it!" Rosebud pointed to a tree that wasn't too far off their path.

High up in a redwood sat a treehouse. The number of stairs that lined either side of the massive tree gave Strelitzia a headache. Did they climb all those? The houses themselves were breathtaking, with elaborate and ornate woodworking decorating each structure. As she kept looking, she noticed that there was more than one house per tree and that each home had its own unique design. Some had carvings of flowers with curling motifs connecting them. Others had what Strelitzia assumed to be letters, possibly family names, along with all kinds of decorations. The one that stood out to Strelitzia had an ocean theme with all different colors of shells, and waves carved into the wood. To her, it was the most beautiful.

The one at the very top was the grandest of them all, far outshining the ones beneath it, and she wondered who lived there. It has the most intricate carvings. Depicting whole pictures, not just small designs. Strelitzia wondered if the levels of the treehouses resembled the classes of the fae, much like their caves back home. Which would mean that residing above everyone else were the royalty of the fae.

Chapter Nine

Nebraria

Strelitzia remained in awe as they continued on their path, not wanting to stray at all out of both respect and a small amount of fear. They watched as the fae carried on with their everyday lives, paying them no mind. She took in the clothing that they wore, the colors of their hair, and the ways in which they moved. They were much more graceful than the goblins. As calm as the fae seemed, Strelitzia wasn't sure how they would react to the goblins diverting from their path.

As they walked, they witnessed the most beautiful sunset, something Strelitzia hadn't seen in a very long time. When she was a little girl, she would climb to the very top of the highest mountain, which put her high above the trees, and she'd watch the sunset. It was one of the most magical moments of her childhood, but she hadn't done it in ages. Her days were no longer as free as they had once been. She now found herself almost always busy with etiquette lessons, royal meetings, and being prepared to rule the settlement.

The sky changed from its bright blue to different shades of yellow, orange, red, and pink, as the sun gradually disappeared from view. In its place, the night sky glistened with stars as the moon beamed with pride. Strelitzia thought she could get used to these views.

"We should probably find somewhere to make camp," Oleander said, after hours of silence, as they all took in their environment.

Strelitzia didn't want to make camp yet. She didn't feel like they had traveled very far, but then she thought of Rosebud and how young goblins need their sleep. She begrudgingly agreed.

"Oh, yeah, sure. Have you seen any caves?" Strelitzia said. The words came out more sarcastic than she had intended, and she hoped Oleander wouldn't notice.

The land here had no mountains. It was primarily flat. Some hills were scattered, but no real mountains that would potentially have caves.

"No, but we can build a tent of some form, I'm sure, among the redwoods," Oleander said.

Strelitzia could detect an eagerness in him. She figured he wanted to show off some of his skills. She wondered if he was feeling restless, not doing anything but walking and occasionally hunting.

"That sounds like a great idea," Strelitzia said, smiling.

"Ooh! Camping!" Rosebud chimed, which made Strelitzia laugh.

"Isn't that what we've been doing every time we've stopped?" Rosebud pondered Strelitzia's question.

"Yeah, I guess you're right. It's still exciting, though." Rosebud beamed as she skipped off toward the forest of redwoods.

Strelitzia glanced around as they made plans to go off their path. She could feel eyes on her but couldn't see where they were.

"Please forgive us if building a tent off our path is forbidden. We mean no disrespect." She spoke softly into the wind, hoping it would reach the ears attached to the prying eyes.

The three gathered everything Oleander said he'd need, and Strelitzia watched as he built an impressive tent. It wasn't large, just big enough for the four of them, but it was still an amazing feat in a land he didn't know. Oleander then built a small fire and excused himself from the group to see what small creatures he could hunt in Nebraria. He soon returned with a couple of rabbits, which he skinned before placing them over the fire to cook.

"Rabbit fur is so soft," Rosebud said. "Why don't we have many rabbits? I've seen pictures of them in books, but I don't think I've ever actually seen one in person."

"I'm not sure, that's a great question though," Strelitzia replied. "We'll have to see what we can find out about that once we return home."

After everyone else was asleep, Strelitzia sat outside the tent, listening to what the wilderness had to say and watching lights twinkle among the trees. It's gentleness when the leaves of the trees swayed. The scurrying of small animals heading home for the night. The occasional hoot of an owl saying goodnight to the moon. The moon itself gleamed brighter here, and Strelitzia found herself tranced by it. It was peaceful here; she had felt no ounce of fear on their whole trek. Even feeling the fae eyes upon her, she didn't fear them. She didn't really want to leave Nebraria. If she could, she'd stay here forever.

The next morning, Strelitzia woke to sounds of clatter above them. She jumped, fearing that the fae were after them for being off their path, and soon they'd be captured, ending their journey. When she got outside the tent, she saw Oleander was already on alert with his face to the treetops. She walked over, glanced at him, and then looked in the direction he was. She saw a fae female walking down the hundreds of stairs, carrying what looked like a tray. She wasn't dressed as nicely as the other fae they'd run into, and her hair was slightly darker and less shiny. Her dress was simple and long, and Strelitzia wondered how she didn't trip heading down all those steps. She assumed it took years of practice to walk in that dress, down those stairs, while carrying a tray. Strelitzia assumed the fae female was coming down from the highest home and watched as she passed a second home before making her way into a third.

Strelitzia and Oleander cleaned up the firepit and the tent while Rosebud and Crocus played with the white daffodils. She watched as the pair swayed to their rhythm. After Strelitzia was satisfied that they'd put everything back to the best of their ability, they continued.

After days of watching the fae carry on with their life, as if the goblins weren't there, they came to a break in the redwoods. Strelitzia looked up to the treetops, studying the elaborate treehouses one more time. She wanted to remember them, always. She decided she'd write about her adventure and wanted to ensure she didn't miss a single detail.

Strelitzia could faintly smell the ocean. They were close, and she smiled. As they made their way through the redwoods, the moss and grass transitioned slowly to warm, soft sand. Strelitzia noticed cliffs in the distance to their left. They looked magnificent, although slightly jagged and dangerous. They looked as though they were standing guard high above the water. Strelitzia wondered if falling from those heights would kill someone. Strelitzia also noticed more redwoods, oddly close to the water. She hadn't thought redwoods could grow that close to water. She looked up and saw by far the largest and most spectacular treehouse she had seen of all. She gaped in awe at the detail not only in the home itself, but also in the stairs.

To their right, she noticed how clean the white sand was. There were shells of all shapes, sizes, and colors scattered everywhere, and seals that were all lying on large rocks, relaxing while sunning themselves. They looked so peaceful, undisturbed. She bent down and picked up a handful of sand

and watched with a smile as the breeze carried it away as she let it go. She closed her eyes and breathed the scent of the ocean deeply, and felt a calm float through her body. When she opened her eyes back up, she caught sight of Oleander, standing near the water. The sun was beaming down on him, making his blue hair and green skin shine. He looked almost God-like. Strelitzia's heart skipped a beat at the sight of him.

Strelitzia then began to panic when she realized Rosebud was not standing among them and began scanning the sand for her. When she spotted her, she sighed with relief. Rosebud was standing with a young fae male deep in conversation by the water's edge. He was dressed nicer than the girl they'd seen coming down the left side staircase. Strelitzia kept her eye on Rosebud and watched their animated conversation unfold. They were laughing, and then they'd get serious, followed by more laughter. There was a bunch of storytelling with their hands. She watched as the young fae pointed up into the treetops. She smiled, wishing interactions with the other creatures and beings of Lurin could be this innocent, this pure. Unlike in the textbooks she'd studied of the arguments and wars between the creatures, there was no arguing, no fighting, just genuine conversation. Soon, Strelitzia watched Rosebud wave goodbye, and she came skipping back to her and Oleander.

"Did you make a friend?" Strelitzia asked her as Rosebud smiled ear to ear.

"I just learned *a lot* from that fae boy! He was really nice. He told me he likes my two-toned hair and that it isn't normal here, and neither is our green skin. He told me all kinds of things about the royal family, including that the king is fat because he won't use the stairs. And how the prince is lazy, well, he used to be, I guess he's different now that he's gotten older. I told him if the prince keeps up with being lazy, then he will probably be fat too, and we both laughed. The fae prince liked to entertain but didn't do a whole lot else. Lots of parties and stuff. He also said that the fae prince would disguise himself and had some super-secret project going, but he was found out by a maid. Can you believe it? A maid! He said the project was a flying contraption. We could fly like Crocus! Wouldn't that be amazing?" Strelitzia giggled at Rosebud's enthusiasm.

"What was his name?" Rosebud's smile shifted to a look of confusion.

Strelitzia watched the strained expression contort her face like she was trying really hard to remember.

"Oh, his name. I don't think I even ask." Strelitzia smiled while she shook her head. "How rude of me!" Rosebud continued, and Strelitzia could tell she felt awful about it. She reached over and put her hands on the small goblin's shoulders.

"It's really ok. Maybe we'll see him on our journey back, and you can ask him then?" Strelitzia smiled, hoping the statement would help Rosebud's mood. Rosebud smiled and nodded before pulling Strelitzia in for a strong hug.

Strelitzia and her group continued the trek across the warm sand, and Strelitzia wanted to take her time. It was warm with a cool breeze coming off the ocean. The smell of salt water danced in the air. She watched as small waves crashed against the shore. It was calming. Before she knew it, they were standing in the water, ankle deep, where the land met the ocean.

Chapter Ten

Open Water

When the group got to the edge of the fae's realm, they were greeted with hundreds of miles of open water standing between them and Thornveil Isle. Strelitzia couldn't see any hints of land in the distance, just open water as far as the eye could see. She looked out to the water, with no idea how to get across. She suddenly didn't want to continue. The fear of the open ocean and the mysteries that lay beneath blossomed in her gut. She glanced over her shoulder, allowing the peace of Nebraria to fill her one more time. She would never forget this land, its beauty and serenity. She already eagerly awaited their return.

"So, any ideas?" Oleander questioned as they all stood listening to the waves crash against the shore and took in the salty ocean air.

"Not entirely, but I think the green crystal could help. I think I could use it to build some form of a boat," Strelitzia responded.

Rosebud sat quietly while the water gently brushed over her feet. She looked to be off in her own little world as she gently ran her hands across and under the warm, soft sand.

"Alright, give it a try," Oleander said with optimism.

Strelitzia did not share his positive outlook, but she appreciated the confidence he had in her. She should've asked Lýsa Crystal more questions about the green crystal. She had no idea what she was doing. She had made trees move out of her way, but would she be able to build a boat? Would she be able to remove trees from where they stand at her bidding?

Strelitzia dug the two crystals out of her bag and held them together in one hand. She gazed down at them, silently hoping that this was going to work. She closed her eyes and pictured what she wanted the crystals to make. Nothing crazy, a wooden boat that would get them across the water. That was it. The crystals began to glow, then the ground began to shake. Hollowed out, tree trunk-sized pieces of wood came hurling out of the ground toward the water. One barely missed Oleander's head. Tree roots and long vines followed, winding themselves around the large pieces of wood. One vine, lined with jasmine flowers, wrapped itself around Rosebud before it made its way to the boat, causing Rosebud to giggle.

"It tickles!" She squealed.

Oleander and Rosebud watched in amazement as Strelitzia crafted a decent-sized boat. After a few minutes, the crystals stopped glowing, and in front of them sat a big enough sailboat for a few people.

The boat was spectacular. It was made entirely of fresh wood, roots, and Jasmine vines. It exuded scents of the fragrant flowers, dirt, and fresh-cut wood. Smells that brought

Strelitzia home. As Strelitzia took in the sight and scent, she began to feel a slight sense of homesickness. She was loving their adventure, spending time with Oleander and Rosebud, and she enjoyed traveling through the realm of the fae, but she was missing home. Missing the smells, the sights, and the security that home provided.

"Let me get on it first and make sure it's sturdy." Oleander headed to the boat without waiting for a response.

Strelitzia admired his protective nature. He would never let anything happen to those he cared about, which left a warm sensation in her heart along with the knowledge that he cared for her deeply.

"We need a sail," Oleander said as he jumped back off the boat. "Otherwise, I think it'll work."

"That should be easy enough; we can make one." Strelitzia jumped into action to find the material they would need to craft a sail. Strelitzia had never actually made anything before, but she'd watched the seamstresses of the settlement and thought it couldn't be that hard.

The three gathered vines, leaves from big leaf maple trees, bark from the redwoods, and moss, and crafted a makeshift sail, securing it to the large mast with twine that Strelitzia had thought could be helpful. Once it was secure, the girls boarded the boat, with Crocus close behind.

Once on board, Strelitzia noticed just how intricate this boat really was. There was immaculate detailing on the railing, and the flowers seemed to be placed in the perfect positions. Oars were resting at the bottom of the boat, four of them. While Strelitzia was deep in thought, admiring the vessel,

Oleander gave it a big push into the water before boarding himself, which made Strelitzia stumble slightly.

Before Strelitzia knew it, they were sailing across the ocean. Strelitzia looked behind them and watched as the land grew smaller and smaller. She had never been in open water and was both excited and worried. Not wanting to dwell too long and stay focused, she turned her attention to her bag and dug out the large map of all the realms of Lurin.

"We need to get to Bloodmist Cove," she announced to Oleander, while pointing to it on the map. "And find the only vampire who will talk to a goblin. He resides in Heedmore, last I knew, and Bloodmist Cover is our best chance of getting there undetected." Strelitzia gazed up at Oleander, waiting for a reply.

"*Blood*mist Cove? That name sounds scary," Rosebud said as she leaned over the side of the boat, putting her hands in the water. Strelitzia and Oleander snapped their attention to her. Strelitzia had assumed that the combination of Crocus and the water would have kept Rosebud preoccupied long enough for them to discuss their next move.

"It is." Strelitzia confirmed, not wanting to lie to the small goblin, "It's their most dangerous port to get to, but it's also our best chance at quickly finding this vampire. We will just need to cover our ears and our skin as best as we can. These vampires think we're greedy mead stupid. They aren't dangerous, though; they won't try to kill us or anything. At least, I don't think they will."

"They don't need to think we're greedy; we *are* a little greedy." Rosebud continued with a giggle. "Have you seen some of the goblins' collections of all things gold?" Strelitzia and Oleander paid her comment and question no mind.

"Then wouldn't it make sense to go to another port and get their kind of cloaks? Don't you think ours will stand out? I highly doubt vampires wear moss." Oleander made a good point and suggestion, but Strelitzia didn't like it.

"How would we get through the shops or vendors that they have? We'd stand out. None of them would give us the time of day. Sure, I brought some gold coins for the venom, but not an abundance. All we have are trivial things that they might not even want." Strelitzia was growing annoyed.

"Trivial gold things. Everyone loves gold." Rosebud chimed.

"How do you know all this?" Oleander finally asked Strelitzia, ignoring Rosebud's comment.

"The royal cave has a secret library. In it, there are books about the other realms." Strelitzia said it so nonchalantly that it made Oleander's jaw drop.

"Don't you think that's information everyone should have access to, not just the royals?" Strelitzia noticed the annoyance in Oleander's tone.

His comment left her speechless. She hadn't thought it would be important for everyone to know the ins and outs of the other realms. The past battles, hostilities, and arguments. The potential threats that loom over Lumiara. The military generals, maybe, sure, but common citizens? It would only leave them in a dudgeon. Why would he want that for the settlement? Why would he want people to be paranoid?

"The books in that library are filled not only with details about the other realms but also with the threats that they pose to us. Ancient battles, arguments. They've been kept secret for centuries to protect the lower-class goblins and ensure they live a stress-free life. None of the previous royals divulged the information, and I don't plan on doing it either. All that would cause is panic. The goblins that need to know, know, and have been sworn to secrecy. Which is what I expect out of you all now." Oleander held his hands up in surrender. Although he still looked angry and annoyed.

"Fine, princess," Oleander responded sarcastically with a bow.

Strelitzia could feel her anger bubble in her gut. "I told you not to call me that."

All the time she'd known him, she hated it when he would flip and treat her as royalty and not as his friend. She didn't want him to treat her that way; he was the one goblin who treated her normally. Not like she was some priceless artifact that needed to be handled gently. She also especially hated being called *"princess"*. She didn't mind being called princess by other goblins, but Oleander made it sound so derogatory.

"Who's going to hear me out here? We're in the middle of the ocean, surrounded only by water. Who is going to hear me?" He yelled at Strelitzia. Rosebud covered her ears. "Ahhhhh!" He continued yelling with his arms raised high into the air.

Strelitzia rushed to him, covering his mouth, "Have you gone mad? Mermaids or worse, Sirens! A kraken! Or maybe a sea monster of some other form that we don't even know about. Had you not thought about what could be *under* the water? Yes, we know about all the different creatures *above* the water, but no one knows anything that lurks in the ocean's depths. Please tell me you're not that stupid. There's no telling what lies beneath these waves." Strelitzia let the hushed, panicked words explode from her mouth before she could really think about what she was saying.

Her eyes grew as she released Oleander. "I'm sorry. That was harsh." She said calmly, trying to steady her rapidly beating heart.

"Yeah," Oleander said before he turned his back on Strelitzia and made his way to the opposite end of the boat. Strelitzia's heart sank watching him walk away from her. She hadn't meant to hurt him.

"I don't like fighting," Rosebud said, not removing her attention from the water that rushed by the boat as they glided through it. "My parents fight a lot. I always hide in my bed when they do. I think they wait until they believe I'm asleep, but I still hear it all. They aren't exactly quiet about it."

"I'm so sorry, I didn't know. Your parents are always so nice to me. We weren't fighting, though, just a little argument between friends." Strelitzia said to her as she made her way to Rosebud's side and wrapped her arms around her in a sturdy embrace.

"That's because of who you are. You're not low-class like we are. They're nice on the outside, not so nice on the inside." Hearing Rosebud's words made Strelitzia wonder just how well she actually knew the goblins in their settlement. Were things going on behind closed doors that no one knew about? Were fellow goblins in despair without her knowledge? Strelitzia made a mental note to look into this upon their return to the Lumiara Mountains and see if she could somehow fix these situations.

Chapter Eleven

Hafgufa

"How much longer?" Rosebud complained as she lay starfished in the middle of the boat while Oleander and Strelitzia rowed.

"I'd like to think we're at least halfway," Strelitzia responded.

"But you don't know that?" Rosebud continued, as she rolled to her stomach and propped her head in her hands to gaze at Strelitzia.

"I don't know for sure, no. I've never crossed the ocean before."

"Well, what I know is that the sun is at its peak in the sky, which means it's time for food." Oleander chimed in as he set down his oar and pulled a long piece of twine with a hook on the end out of his pack.

Strelitzia watched as Oleander tossed the line into the water, sat down, and started to hum.

"What is he doing?" Rosebud whispered to Strelitzia.

"Fishing." Rosebud's eyes grew wide at Strelitzia's response.

"Goblins actually do that? With something other than their hands?" Strelitzia looked at Rosebud, bewildered by her question.

"How do you get fish from the stream?" Strelitzia was genuinely curious. She had only known of fishing to retrieve anything from the water with a hook and twine. She was now assuming there was a lot about the lower class that she did not know. Her intense hunger for knowledge blossomed within her.

"Hands and buckets. The men make traps out of buckets to catch them, and then they use their hands to yank them from the traps, and then they smash their fists onto their heads against large rocks to kill them." Rosebud told the whole story while she made all the necessary motions with her own hands.

As Strelitzia watched Rosebud tell her story, she smiled but also flinched when she motioned the beating of the fish. She really enjoyed talking with this young goblin. The innocence in her voice and eyes was refreshing.

"Well, that's," Strelitzia was at a loss for words. What she wanted to say was that it sounded savage. Was there no form of elegance in the lower class? She really didn't know much about how the other half lived. "Interesting," was the best she could come up with.

Rosebud smiled, then shifted her attention to Crocus, who was lying on the railing of the boat, sunbathing. After a few painfully boring moments, Oleander had caught enough fish for the four of them. Strelitzia was intrigued as Oleander skinned, cleaned, and, with Crocus's helpful flame, cooked the fish, handing one to each member on the boat.

Strelitzia gazed out into the water and thought she could see a small island, covered in hills, in the distance. It looked lush and beautiful, full of trees and bright green grass. She thought they could stop there and take a break to stretch their sea legs. The thought made her smile. They'd only been on the boat for a little over a day, and she was already over its rocking. She was ready to be on hard land.

"How would you all feel about stopping on that island for a bit? Get out of the boat and off the water for the night?" The others nodded, and Strelitzia smiled as she took another bite out of her fish.

As they ate, the clouds began to grow dark, casting a deep shadow over the water, and the wind began to pick up. As rain began to fall, Strelitzia knew they were in for a storm.

"What was that?" Rosebud asked, as she pointed to something far from the ship.

Oleander and Strelitzia moved to her position staring out across the open water, but saw nothing. The water was starting to wave and swirl, and a mist began to rise from the water's surface. Strelitzia stood confused. Where did the island go? It was there just a moment ago.

"Well, that can't be good," Oleander said. "Is it my turn to show how not stupid I am?" Strelitzia felt the intended jab; she sighed heavily and rolled her eyes. She couldn't believe he still hadn't gotten over their argument. It was almost a full day ago, and she had apologized three times.

"It's a storm. What's to know?" Strelitzia responded as sweetly as she could. She wanted the tension between them to end. She wanted the sweet, thoughtful, protective Oleander back. She was not a fan of this side of him.

"That wasn't an island you saw. It was Hafgufa," Oleander said. Strelitzia looked at Rosebud, who shared her confused expression.

"What is that?" Rosebud asked with a trembling voice.

No sooner did the question escape Rosebud's mouth, there was a loud splash from behind them, and a dark mass swiftly moved its way toward their boat. The island that had once been so close to them, now gone. Strelitzia was terrified by the sight of an enormous tail gliding its way back into the water through the mile-high sprays of the splash.

"Hafgufa is a huge and terrifying beast that lives in the ocean's depths. It is a monstrous whale-like creature that disguises itself as an island. Legend says Hafgufa can cause dangerous storms and whirlpools that engulf entire ships." Rosebud burst into tears as soon as Oleander finished his speech.

"We're going to die!" Rosebud whaled.

Strelitzia smacked her palm to her forehead as she rolled her eyes again. How could Oleander say something so bluntly in front of a young goblin? Although she feared the worst, she would never let that on to Rosebud. Strelitzia took a deep breath to calm the annoyance that was lingering in her soul.

"Good going, Oleander," Strelitzia said, narrowing her eyes at him.

"We're not going to die, we're going to be just fine." Strelitzia tried her best to comfort Rosebud, although she was just as scared. She gripped Rosebud into a hug and could feel her small body tremble against her. Her heart was beating rapidly in her chest.

"Don't lie to her. You don't *know* that." Strelitzia shot Oleander a look that told him to shut up. Hadn't he realized he'd already scared poor little Rosebud enough?

"You are going to make a great father someday," Strelitzia said condescendingly, and she hugged Rosebud. Strelitzia wondered if that would be a deal breaker for her, him potentially being a bad father. She thought back on her time with her father and, although he wasn't warm and fuzzy, she did have good memories with him. Didn't all parents slip up every once in a while, though? Maker knows her parents weren't perfect.

They watched in horror as a whirlpool started to form only a few feet in front of them. Rosebud screamed, and Crocus took off into the sky towards the boat's sail.

"What do we do, mister know-it-all?" Strelitzia yelled to Oleander over the deafening sounds of the wind and thunder.

"Hold on tight?" Strelitzia narrowed her eyes at Oleander. She had to come up with a plan.

"We need to reroute the boat. Oleander, help me!" She yelled as she made her way for an oar. Rosebud followed, also grabbing an oar. Once all three were seated, they started rowing as hard as they could to attempt to turn the boat away from the whirlpool.

Strelitzia noticed Rosebud looking out into the water, terror holding firm in the young goblin's eyes, freezing her in a trance. She watched intently as Rosebud slowly stopped rowing and made her way to the edge of the boat.

"Rosebud!" Strelitzia yelled after her, not letting up on her rowing, "Come back over here! Get away from the edge!" but Rosebud didn't seem to hear her.

Strelitzia watched helplessly as Rosebud reached her small hand into the water and gently swayed it beneath the ocean's surface. As she did, the whirlpool started to grow smaller. Oleander and Strelitzia froze. As Rosebud continued, the giant dark mass beneath the waves started making its way to the surface, until its head was directly under Rosebud's hand. It was huge. Much larger than any creature Strelitzia had ever seen. It towered stories above their small boat, making it look like a toy.

"Hello," Rosebud said to the creature.

As it continued to rise from out of the water, it made the boat tilt and sway. As it peered down, Strelitzia's heart sank as her eyes grew wide and fear consumed her. The pure white eyes of Hafgufa sent a chill down Strelitzia's spine. She watched in terror as it opened its mouth wide, revealing row upon row of sharp, jagged teeth. It let out a powerful, foul-smelling belch, sending their boat sailing across the water at high speed. They all squinted as the stench burned their eyes. Strelitzia fell to the ground along with the others, sending a sharp pain radiating through the arm she landed on, as the boat was launched across the water. As Hafgufa slammed its cavernous jaw closed, a giant wave headed their way, pushing the boat faster and further. The sharpness of the jolt knocked them all down again. Strelitzia hit her head on the floor of the boat. Soon, Strelitzia succumbed to pure darkness.

Strelitzia's eyes fluttered open. What happened? The last thing she remembered was the monstrous Hafgufa attacking their boat. She stood slowly and saw that Oleander, Rosebud, and Crocus were all fast asleep or potentially still knocked out. She surveyed the boat, feeling for small cracks or holes, checking to make sure the wood was still smooth. She inspected the sail for rips or tears, but she found nothing. It appeared to be in good condition. There were no leaks, no holes anywhere, everything was still miraculously intact, and they were now calmly sailing. Strelitzia remained confused. From what Oleander had been saying, they should all be dead. A sense of relief washed over her as she checked her pulse to make sure she was, in fact, alive.

She grabbed their water canteen that had been thrown across the ship and took a swig from it. She glanced around at the mess that was now aboard their boat with them. Provisions, pieces of fur they'd gathered, maps, and weapons were tossed everywhere. She took a deep breath. What a mess. Before she could start gathering all their belongings and put them back where they belonged, she noticed land not too far in front of them. Her eyes widened at the realization of where they were. Hafgufa cut their journey practically in half. Before her was Thornveil Isle, home of the vampires.

Chapter Twelve

Thornveil Isle

"Thornveil Isle," Oleander announced after he had finally come to.

"But that can't be Bloodmist Cove," Strelitzia said, sounding concerned.

"Look!" Rosebud yelled as she pointed toward the docks. Strelitzia, with Crocus now resting on her shoulder, and Oleander made their way to Rosebud's side.

"Is that a statue of a goblin?" Oleander questioned.

"It is! It looks like you, Strelitzia!" The excitement in Rosebud's voice did not resonate in Strelitzia.

Did they know about her? Was this a trap? Dread bubbled inside, but oddly, there was also anger. Nothing in the books she'd read said anything about a goblin statue. She pressed her temples, attempting to prevent a headache.

"Oleander, a word, please?" Strelitzia said to him casually.

She was tired of their bickering and his avoidance of her. Strelitzia moved herself to the back of the boat, with Oleander on her heels.

"I don't know what needs to be done or said, but I want this bickering between us to stop." Oleander stood motionless and expressionless with his arms crossed against his chest, which gave Strelitzia little hope.

"I just need time." He finally responded.

"Time isn't exactly something we have a whole lot of at the moment. We could be walking into significant *danger*, and I need to know that we're okay. I need to know that you have my back." There was urgency in Strelitzia's voice. They were rapidly approaching the home of all vampires, and she was unsure how Oleander was feeling. Would he let her be eaten by one of those blood thirsty varmints?

"I'm aware. Look, even though we argued, that doesn't mean it changed how I feel for you or my ability to protect both you and Rosebud. I just need some time to wrap my head around the things you said. Although you've apologized for them, I know you wouldn't have come up with that just to hurt me. It's how you really felt. Anger tends to bring out the truth." Strelitzia's heart melted. That wasn't how she actually felt. Regret clouded her every thought.

"Oleander, that's not how I really feel." She reached out and placed her hand on his chest. His heartbeat was soothing against her palm. "I was angry, and I made a mistake and said something that I shouldn't have. That's all it was, and I truly hope that you can forgive me. I care about you more than I could ever speak." She felt tears forming in her eyes with every word.

"Okay. Then just give me time." Then Oleander walked away, leaving Strelitzia to drown in her regret.

The closer Strelitzia and the others got to Crimsonreach Crossing, the louder it got. Music wafted through the air, along with laughter and conversation. People yelling from their vendor tents, trying to get anyone to buy what they had. Strelitzia noticed that there were docks for multiple creatures: goblins, fae, pirates, and the like. Maybe this wasn't a trap. Maybe Strelitzia had this place all wrong. Maybe everything they knew about vampires was incorrect. Or, maybe, it was all old. Maybe now things were different. Strelitzia didn't know how to handle this. She had believed that vampires hated them for so long that being here now, seeing her surroundings, she was dumbfounded. She felt a steady wave of calm wash over her, amidst the questions that plagued her mind.

They pulled up to the dock, adorned with the goblin statue. Oleander got out and tied up the boat. There was no one there to greet them, which Strelitzia found odd. She took in their surroundings as they walked up the dock towards the town. The land was covered in trees, jasmine vines covered the stone arch at the end of the pier, and random patches of wildflowers were growing. It reminded her of home.

"Hey, look, a pub for goblins," Oleander exclaimed before racing off to it, with Rosebud close behind. Strelitzia kept her pace, still hesitant about the new place.

"The Goblin Watering Hole. Original," Strelitzia said, as she finally made her way to the pub. She couldn't help but feel nervous about their current situation. Why was all this here?

When she walked in, Oleander and Rosebud were already sitting at a table with drinks and a plate of food in front of them. She watched as they clanked their wooden mugs and downed the contents. She shook her head.

"We really don't have time for this. I don't want to waste time on frivolous things. We're here for a purpose." She said quietly to her companions. Crocus fluttered from her shoulder to the table and practically threw his entire body into Oleander's mug.

"We've been at sea for days. We deserve this. We did something no other goblin has ever done." Oleander ranted.

"Really? Obviously, other goblins have been here. Why do you think that statue and this pub exist here? Also, now we don't actually know if any of the goblins in our settlement's history have been here. You don't think it odd that that statue resembles me?" Rosebud and Oleander looked at each other and shrugged.

"What I know is that we aren't in danger here. Did you look around outside before you came in?" Oleander questioned. Strelitzia had, but barely. Not like Oleander apparently had. She was taking in her surroundings, yes, but not the people.

"Fine. You two stay here. I'll be back." Strelitzia said, full of frustration.

"No. No," Oleander said, as he put up a hand. "Have one drink, and then we will all go. We will stick together. Besides, Rosebud was hungry, and we all needed to battle off our sea legs. Sit." Strelitzia couldn't argue that.

She reluctantly sat down and was greeted by a human who dropped off a mug for her with a smile. A smile? Humans hated goblins. Why was she smiling?

"Better, yeah?" Oleander asked her as he gently placed his hand on top of Strelitzia's, sending a spark racing through her hand and arm. She took just a minute to glance into Oleander's eyes and watch them sparkle. The attraction she had for this goblin was growing more and more, day by day.

Once they were done, they ventured into the depths of Crimsonreach Crossing. Strelitzia became instantly overwhelmed. Crimsonreach was flooded with vendors, pubs, and merchants yelling into the crowd. There were bright colors everywhere, which hurt her eyes. Walking among them were all the creatures with a designated port. As they roamed, Strelitzia felt Crocus stiffen.

"What is it?" Strelitzia asked him before remembering he was unable to speak. She sifted through her bag and found her potion for him. She popped the cork, and he gently breathed in the puff that came from the bottle. Strelitzia had never seen him be gentle about that.

"Strelitzia," he said calmly, "they are selling dragon-flies." He made himself as small as he could and tried to hide within Strelitzia's long purple hair.

She glanced around and noticed one vendor in particular had cage upon cage of dragon-flies. They were all different colors, and they all looked miserable. The cages that held them weren't even big enough for them to stretch their wings, and they all had tiny muzzles across their snouts. Strelitzia felt a knife flow straight through her heart, looking at all these poor creatures. Her heart broke for them. Who could do this? They never harmed anyone. With anger, she made her way to the vendor.

"Where did you get these dragon-flies?" Strelitzia demanded.

The vendor laughed. "Why do you want one? It seems you've already got one. How about another? I can sell you one for a good price." Strelitzia was disgusted.

"How much for them all?" She asked impatiently.

"All? Are you serious?"

"Yes. But also, how much for you to never capture and sell a dragon-fly again?" The vendor laughed at her and ignored her question completely.

Strelitzia became annoyed that he hadn't responded, and so easily moved on to the next customer. She wanted to yell that she was the Princess of the Lumiara Mountains and that he *would* do as she says, but that would be foolish. That could potentially put them in harm's way, so she kept her mouth shut.

"Come on. We will find a way to free them," Oleander whispered to her. "We need to find vampire venom so we can get out of here." Strelitzia nodded, and they continued.

They passed so many different vendors, and they all made Strelitzia sick. One had caged phoenixes, another was selling unicorn horns and geminox gems, while some had simpler things like fruits and bread.

"Strelitzia!" Rosebud squealed. "Can I get this? Please!" Strelitzia looked at what was in the little goblin's hand. It appeared to be some sort of stone.

"What is it?" She asked,

"That would be a philosopher's stone. It's an alchemical substance that changes base metals into gold. Very rare." The vendor told her.

"Does it actually work?" Strelitzia asked.

"Well, if you buy it, you can find that out for yourself. Or you could play my little game and possibly win it for free." Strelitzia was confused. Was this common behavior here?

"Oh, Strelitzia, can I play the game, please?" Rosebud asked.

"We don't even know what the game is," Strelitzia said to Rosebud.

"It's rather simple. I place this blue marble under one of these three cups, and you just follow the cup and then tell me which cup it's under after I mix them around." The vendor was doing his best to entice Strelitzia to play his game.

"Alright, go ahead, Rosebud," Strelitzia said. Rosebud beamed as she squealed with excitement.

"I love games!" Rosebud yelled.

"Alright, follow the marble! This way, that way, where did the marble go? Follow, follow, or you'll never know!" Strelitzia watched intently as he shuffled the cups all over the table, keeping a keen eye on the cup with the marble. "Alright, young goblin, it's time to pick your cup!"

Strelitzia watched as Rosebud raised a finger to her chin, appearing to be deep in thought. After a minute, Rosebud smiled a mischievous little grin that made Strelitzia proud, although she wasn't sure why.

"The left one," Rosebud said with utmost confidence. Strelitzia agreed with her choice.

The vendor raised the left mug, and sitting beneath it was the shiny blue marble. The vendor laughed, "Best two out of three?" Rosebud opened her mouth to respond, but Strelitzia cut her off.

"Actually, we're in a hurry. We'll take the philosopher's stone and be on our way."

"That'll be five gold coins." The vendor replied.

"I'm sorry? You said if she won your game, she'd get it for free." Strelitzia didn't understand. Rosebud played his game, Rosebud won, but why wasn't he handing over this stone?

"You didn't do two out of three." The vendor shrugged. Strelitzia rolled her eyes, fully annoyed with this human. She pulled five gold coins out of her bag and slammed them onto his table, causing the entire thing to shake.

"Here. And they call *us* greedy." Strelitzia sneered at the human, showing vaguely her sharply filed teeth. The vendor swallowed hard and handed the stone to Rosebud.

"You all have a nice day." He said timidly. Very different from the haggler Strelitzia had just been dealing with.

"Thank you!" Rosebud squealed. Seeing her so happy made Strelitzia's anger subside, replaced with happiness.

"Look at that, your first purchase at Crimsonreach," Oleander said playfully as he placed his arm around Strelitzia's shoulder. Her heart fluttered.

"Does this mean you forgive me?" Strelitzia said with hope.

"Yeah," Oleander stated with a smile, which Strelitzia returned.

"Thank goodness. We need to find vampire venom. It doesn't appear any of these vendors have it." Strelitzia started to feel defeated.

"Vampire venom, you say?" A male voice said from behind them. Strelitzia whipped around and was face-to-face with a human. The man wore a strange-looking suit and had boring brown hair. His teeth, however, were too white and took up most of his face, which had a trimmed beard covering his chin. He was horrendous to look at. "My name is Lord Beaumont, and I have what you seek."

Strelitzia eyed him curiously. "What do you want for it?"

"Ten gold coins." He tried to dazzle Strelitzia with his smile, but failed. She only found him more repulsive. His teeth were flat; what good would that do?

"We'll give you five." Oleander chimed in. Oleander was at least a foot taller than this Lord Beaumont, which made Strelitzia laugh. It almost looked like this guy was going to soil himself.

Lord Beaumont laughed, "No negotiations. It's ten coins. Take it or leave it." Oleander looked down at Strelitzia and waited for her to take the lead.

She had brought plenty of coins with her. She hadn't known how much she would need, so she knew she'd be able to afford it. She looked at Lord Beaumont and his smug grin and felt her stomach churn. She was unsure about this *Lord*.

"Tell me more about it," Strelitzia finally said.

"Of course. This is the Tinsdale family's venom. The best of the best." Strelitzia had never heard the name Tinsdale. She wanted the venom from the Everthorne family.

"I heard Everthorne venom was the *best of the best.*" Strelitzia fired back. She watched as the wheels turned in Lord Beaumont's head, if only for a split second.

"It used to be, yes. However, now, it's the Tinsdale venom that works far better than any of the rest." He held the vial out in front of Strelitzia. She stared at it. It didn't feel right, but what did she know about vampire venom, really?

"Okay. We'll take it." She told him as she fished out ten gold coins and handed them over to the human.

"Pleasure doing business with you." Then he was gone. Melting into the sea of people and creatures that crowded the streets, never to be seen again.

Strelitzia stared at the vial she held in her hand. It didn't look right. From the way it had been described in the book about Thornveil Isle, she assumed it would be shinier. She shrugged her shoulders and put it safely in her pack.

"Let's find somewhere to stay for the night," she said to Oleander and Rosebud, while Crocus was doing small loops off of Strelitzia's shoulder.

Chapter Thirteen

Knockoff Venom

Strelitzia and the others walked a while longer, stopping to get some snacks and other small trinkets to remember their grand adventure. Strelitzia watched as Rosebud strolled without a care, skipping as she went. She felt the presence of Oleander by her side every step, which made it all the easier to breathe and remain calm. Crocus sat on Strelitzia's shoulder, and she could feel his tiny claws digging into her skin. When she glanced over at him, his little nose was going crazy from all the smells that lingered. The colors were vibrant and breathtaking in the sun, and it made Strelitzia wonder if the colors of her own settlement would be as wondrous if the sun were able to peek through the treetops.

Soon, they came to a lodging house. It looked inviting enough. It had a sign hanging by the large door that said 'vacancy' with flowerpots on either side. The door itself was a solid wood with a black wrought iron handle. Strelitzia glanced up and saw multiple rows of windows cracked open with curtains flowing in the breeze. She walked in and was greeted by a couple of couches, small tables, and a large desk. Behind it were rows of keys and an unhappy-looking human who was flipping through the pages of a book.

"Hello, we'd like a room, please." The lady behind the counter appeared bored and handed her a key without a single word. Strelitzia looked down at the key and saw there was no indication of which room it belonged to.

"Excuse me, but which room?" Strelitzia asked as politely as she could.

The lady rolled her eyes.

"Room four, down the hall on the right." She sounded exasperated.

"Thank you." Strelitzia hadn't experienced such rudeness, and it made her a bit angry.

When they walked into the room, Strelitzia first noticed the large window on the opposite wall that overlooked the main street in Crimsonreach. There was a small fireplace and only two beds with little tables on either side and in between. It was against the goblin royal protocol for Strelitzia to share a bed with anyone other than her husband, but it would be more inappropriate for Oleander to share a bed with young Rosebud. So, she broke the rules, again, and decided she'd share a bed with Rosebud.

"Crocus, do you want to try this now? Or wait until morning?" Crocus puffed sparks out of his tiny nose and started doing small spins all over the floor. Strelitzia and Rosebud laughed.

"I think that means now, Litza." Strelitzia looked at her, confused. No one had ever given her a nickname before. That wasn't proper. She liked it, though.

Strelitzia retrieved the two vials from her bag and scrutinized them both. She didn't want to use her entire vial for the test, just in case something went wrong. She found a glass and put a little of the vampire venom into it. She glanced at the vial of vampire venom and thought that it would look different. It had been said that it really shone and was almost mesmerizing, but this one seemed lackluster. She grew skeptical of this particular vial of venom but decided to hope for the best.

"Alright, Crocus, you're going to have to make this quick. The smoke is going to come and go quickly with an opening this size." Crocus flew his way to the rim of the glass and perched himself there, almost tipping it over. As small as he was, he wasn't quite small enough not to tip over a glass.

Strelitzia carefully poured a small amount of her potion into the glass and watched as the two liquids mixed. Creating an ethereal, glimmering green swirl. A puff of smoke escaped the mixture, and Crocus quickly flew around breathing it all in. When he sat back at the table, the three goblins stared at him and waited.

"So," Strelitzia started, "How do you feel?"

"I don't know. Fine, I guess." He wasn't rambling; that was a good sign. At least, Strelitzia thought it was.

"Do you feel fuzzy?" Rosebud asked. Strelitzia looked at her curiously. Her potion had never made Crocus feel fuzzy; she figured the young goblin just wanted to be included.

"No. I feel fine. I don't feel the crazy jitters that I normally do." Crocus continued.

"Alright, I guess now we wait and see how long it lasts," Strelitzia said.

Strelitzia sat in their room the rest of the night. She was amazed by how comfortable the beds were. The thick pads outshone the layers of moss that they used on their stone beds. Rosebud almost instantly fell asleep after they'd eaten a meal of bread, fruit, and dried meat. Oleander passed out shortly after. Strelitzia, though, stayed up for a few hours more just talking with Crocus. Around midnight, the potion wore off. It lasted only a few minutes longer than it typically does. Strelitzia felt defeated. This was supposedly the strongest vampire venom. She was now even more skeptical of what that Lord guy had said. She decided, in the morning, instead of heading home, they'd be making the journey to Bloodmist Cove.

Chapter Fourteen

Icebergs

Strelitzia woke the next morning before the sun. Before Oleander. Before Rosebud. Before Crocus, which wasn't really a surprise. She made her way to the window in their room and looked out over Crimsonreach. The chaos hadn't started yet. The vendors were still setting up for their day. It was the calm before the storm.

She still couldn't believe that they were there. She had done what she wanted to do, almost. She had left her settlement and had been exploring the realms. Along the way, she had realized that she had also been developing strong feelings for Oleander, which continued to grow. Yes, she had always had them somewhere deep down; she just chose to ignore them. However, now, she felt as though she couldn't any longer. He blindly agreed to go with her on her journey, and that is something she knew she'd never be able to thank him enough for.

Strelitzia contemplated how they would get to Bloodmist Cove. Obviously, everything she had read about vampires was wrong. The vampires didn't care about them. Yes, vampires saw them as greedy, but in a way, so were they. They wanted money and gold just as much as the goblins had. So much so that the vampires and humans welcomed all types of creatures into Crimsonreach.

Strelitzia went and pulled out her map to find the best route to Bloodmist Cove, and she decided that it would be best to travel by water. But she worried about the conditions of the water off the coast of Bloodmist Cove, though. If it were true, and her map wasn't lying to her, it was riddled with icebergs. She wondered if the green crystal could help with those. She knew it could manipulate earth, but what about water and ice? Were those considered part of earth? She decided she would risk it and find out. The worst that could happen would be that it just doesn't work.

While deep in thought, Strelitzia heard Oleander stir. It was time for them to go.

"Good morning," She announced. She received a grunt in response. She watched as he sleepily sat himself up.

"It's too early," Oleander mumbled, still half asleep, his eyes still closed.

"We need to get moving. We need to get to Bloodmist Cove. That man lied to us. This venom is awful. It didn't work." Strelitzia began to wonder if that was actually true. Or, if the man was right, and this was the most potent form of vampire venom. She had to believe it wasn't. Otherwise, this was all for nothing. Maybe not entirely for nothing, though, she had gone on her grand adventure. The adventure she had yearned for.

Strelitzia got the others motivated and, together, they made their way back to the ship, but not before stopping and having a warm, hearty breakfast.

"How far to Bloodmist Cove?" Oleander asked Strelitzia as he prepared the boat. Strelitzia watched as his muscles moved and strained, getting the sail back to its rightful place. Something stirred in her that made her nervous and caused unladylike thoughts. She shook her head and refocused on his question.

"Going up the coast, it should be about seven hundred miles. We could make it in three days if we don't stop. Maybe we should take turns sleeping so we don't waste time?" Strelitzia questioned Oleander, whose mouth had dropped open.

"Seven hundred miles!? How big is this place?"

"Oh, stop. Lumiara is roughly six hundred miles. It's no different from home." She tried to smile to ease his shock. It didn't work.

"Strelitzia, that's one hundred miles more than home. That's a pretty significant difference." Strelitzia hadn't ever noticed Oleander's vocabulary. It was decently big for a lower-class warrior. She found herself impressed by him. She hadn't known the lower-class goblins to use larger words; they tended to keep it simple. The word *significant* wasn't one that they typically learned.

"What's Bloodmist Cove like? Is it like this place?" Rosebud asked innocently as she made herself comfortable on the boat.

"Not from what I've read, but I'm wondering if we had everything wrong. Bloodmist Cove is dark. Cold. Practically in ruin. It had once been the nicest port in Thornveil Isle; however, it was abandoned with the creation of Crimsonreach. Now, it's said at least, that it's a graveyard of shipwrecks and hope." Rosebud's eyes grew wide with fear.

"And we have to go there?" Rosebud question.

Strelitzia nodded. "Yes, we have to find an Everthorne vampire. They have the best venom." Strelitzia heard Rosebud gulp down a lump in her throat before she turned her attention to the water.

"A few days of mindless floating and we'll be there. It'll be fine." Strelitzia smiled at Oleander's attempts to reassure Rosebud that there was nothing to fear. Strelitzia believed him. She knew that as long as he was around, and they had the crystals to assist them, nothing would harm them.

"Are we there yet?" Rosebud asked after almost two days of sailing with no problems. The trip so far had been rather uneventful and quicker than Strelitzia had expected.

They watched the coast and made sure to keep it in sight, so they didn't stray too far into the depths of the ocean. Strelitzia and Oleander had agreed to stay close, so they didn't run into any unexpected water creatures or monsters.

Strelitzia had started to worry about Crocus. He was keeping to himself, which was rarely how he acted. He was a very social little creature who enjoyed being around other beings. Even when he was unable to speak. Ever since Strelitzia had found Crocus, he had been attached to her. His small, blue, and green body with beautiful, tie-dyed wings that shimmered in the sun had always rested on her shoulder.

"Crocus!" Strelitzia yelled, hoping the small dragon-fly would hear her.

He made his way to her, landing gently in front of her.

Strelitzia knelt to him, pulling out her vial. She popped the cork, and he very slowly inhaled the puff of green that escaped from the bottle.

"Are you alright?" Strelitzia asked. Her voice dripped with concern.

"Yeah. I guess I just got my hopes up and then they were crushed." The sadness in Crocus's eyes made Strelitzia's heart clench. She wanted nothing more than to help her tiny friend.

"Don't lose hope. We're not giving up yet. This vampire will have the real stuff. I know it." Crocus tried to give Strelitzia a reassuring smile. While she appreciated the gesture, she knew he was now weary of vampire venom.

A chill in the air came from seemingly nowhere. It floated gracefully with the wind, which caused Strelitzia to wrap her moss cloak around her tighter. She looked over at Rosebud, who was asleep, and made her way to her to ensure she was covered and warm. The clouds darkened as did the water. The ocean around them became angry, sending small swells at their boat. Strelitzia knew, in her heart, this meant they were close. Bloodmist Cove had become notorious for the harsh, freezing waters.

"Strelitzia." Hearing Oleander saying her name so nonchalantly, like he was always meant to say it, gave Strelitzia butterflies. "I think we're close." He motioned over the boat's railing.

Not far ahead were the tips of what Strelitzia assumed to be giant icebergs, littered with the remains of old pirate ships. The icebergs looked sharp and gleamed in the few beams of sunlight that fought their way through the dark clouds. Both dangerous and beautiful. She studied them and wondered how big they were beneath the dark blue waves and if their small boat would make it to the shore. She didn't see any docks, but for all she knew, they were long gone, just broken rubble under the water.

"We need to do this strategically," Oleander started. "These icebergs could ruin our chances of being able to get home. If we hit them, we're cooked mosssprites. The temperatures of these waters would freeze us to death quickly. The closer we get, the worse the conditions will get." Strelitzia noticed how he kept his voice low; she assumed he didn't want to wake and scare Rosebud. This gave Strelitzia a glimmer of hope on the *good father* debate that continued in her mind.

"I wish there were a way to see under the water. It had been so clear before." Strelitzia wasn't wrong. It had been crystal clear, blue waters before now. She had been able to see the pebbles and seagrass on the ocean's floor with the small fish swimming through. Now, it was dark and mucky, yet still enchanting.

"You might want to find something to hold onto," Oleander said to her calmly.

Strelitzia made her way to the mast, securing a hemp rope around it. She gently lifted Rosebud and moved her to the center of the boat, tying the rope around her waist. Strelitzia rummaged through her bag until she found the crystals. She gripped them tightly, hoping they'd be able to help if need be.

No sooner did she get the crystals in her hand, the waters started to toss the boat, aiming it dead on for an iceberg. Strelitzia's eyes grew wide before she shut them and gripped the crystals tighter, clinging with all her might to the mast. *Move the iceberg out of our way.* She thought to herself, hoping that they would actually move. When she reopened her eyes, she saw they were still on the fast track to colliding with the iceberg. She started to cry. She brought these two innocent goblins on her journey, and now they would die for that, and it would be all her fault. She gripped the center mast with shaking hands and arms, attempting to brace herself for impact.

Small icicles shot up from the waves as if something had a bow under the water, piercing their sail and the sides of the boat. Strelitzia screamed, as did Rosebud, who had just been woken by an icicle getting too close. Crocus was perched on Rosebud, using his flames to melt them before they reached them, and Oleander was ducking and dodging anything thrown his way. Strelitzia started to panic. With every moment, they were one inch closer to sure death. Chilling water began to coat the bottom of the boat, freezing their hide-covered feet. These waters would be their graves.

She looked over the edge of the boat and was horrendously greeted by a floating skull that she assumed had once belonged to a pirate. She tried not to focus on it and refocused on the land that was still not too far off. If they could just get to land, they'd be alright.

"Oleander, head inland!" She yelled over the howl of the wind. Oleander quickly shifted the direction of the boat. He shoved two oars into the water and leaned all his body weight on the side of the boat, barely missing an iceberg's tip.

Strelitzia clung to the crystals so hard that the Lýsa Crystal shard cut the palm of her hand. She could feel the blood pooling. *I just want to get to land.* She thought to herself on repeat. Amongst the chaos of the stormy waters, the jasmine vines began to rumble and detach from the boat. Strelitzia watched in amazement as they shot themselves off the boat and toward land, growing, multiplying, and intertwining themselves into sturdy ropes. The vines dove under the water, moving swiftly beneath the waves, shot up on land, and secured themselves to what was left of a stone pillar. They pulled the boat along with them. The boat itself avoided each iceberg and any debris.

Strelitzia was stunned further that the boat was repairing itself. Any hole from ice ripping through its sides was quickly mended. Any rips to the sail were rapidly sewn. The boat dashed through the water at an incredibly high speed until it crashed into the icy ground of Bloodmist Cove.

Chapter Fifteen

Bloodmist Cove

The stories Strelitzia had read about Bloodmist Cove did not disappoint. This place was a wasteland of a forgotten time. The docks had been thrashed by the icy water. Stone pillars and walls lay in rubble on the cold, hard ground. Statues had been beaten by the harsh weather, some to practically nothing. Remnants of ships that lost their battles with the icebergs had washed up onto shore. The entire scene was a loud cry for help. The clouds above them were almost black, casting an unnatural shadow over what had once been a lively place, turned to a graveyard of despair. This is what Strelitzia thought of when she thought about vampires. Not someplace as lively and colorful as Crimsonreach Crossing. But somewhere dark, cold, dying, and dead, like Bloodmist Cove.

Strelitzia glanced back at the water as she stood on what was left of one of the docks. She watched as the icebergs taunted her. They threatened her eventual return to the ocean.

Their menacing moans as they shifted in the water echoed through the wind.

"Well, this is lovely," Oleander said sarcastically as he approached Strelitzia's side. "Are you sure about this?"

Strelitzia wasn't entirely sure she had made the right call. She had started to regret making this journey by water and wondered if heading to Heedmore by land would've been the safer option. Of course it was, she wasn't dumb. She had opted for quick, not careful.

"Yes, we just have to head west, and we will reach Heedmore. From there, we will find this Everthorne vampire, and then we can go home. Heedmore shouldn't be far from here. We just should move quickly." Strelitzia tried to sound reassuring and positive, but the doom and gloom of the atmosphere was making that difficult. She felt a chill crawl across her skin at the thought of being in this desolate place. She clenched her jaw and her fists, attempting to fight off both the chill and the fear.

"And what makes you think this vampire will just hand over vampire venom to you?" Oleander raised a good point.

Yes, she'd brought gold, but she didn't actually know if that would be enough or if that's what vampires wanted.

"I don't like this," Rosebud announced from behind Strelitzia and Oleander, clutching her arms around herself, with Crocus by her side.

Strelitzia and Oleander made their way toward the small goblin and gazed at what stood only a few feet before them. A forest. A dark, dying forest. The trees in front of them had no leaves, and their branches looked as though they'd reach down and snatch them up. With the help of the wind off the ocean, they rustled together, almost like they were shaking hands, creating a scratchy sound that made your ears bleed. Strelitzia felt uneasy at the sight and sounds of this forest and deeply hoped that there was a way around them. The thought of having to go into the forest of dead trees terrified her greatly. The fear she had just been trying to push away came back with vengeance.

Strelitzia felt something drip on her foot, and she froze. When she looked down, she saw a single droplet of hot pink blood. She raised her hand to see a deep, bleeding gash from the Lýsa Crystal shard. She panicked.

"Dang it," Strelitzia said, her voice frantic as she threw herself and her bag to the ground.

"What is it?" Oleander asked, without looking. His stare remained on the menacing forest in front of them.

"I'm bleeding." She rummaged through her bag quickly, forgetting the dreaded forest in front of her, and started looking for her wound kit. She had remembered to pack it, didn't she?

"Great time to be bleeding," Oleander said with equal panic in his tone. "No telling what bloodthirsty vampires are here." Strelitzia gave him a mean side eye and pulled some yarrow leaves and aloe out of her bag.

"Can we please not with the sarcasm right now? I'm just as terrified as you are." Strelitzia snapped back at him.

She ripped open the aloe leaf and let the slimy contents pour over her wound. Once she was satisfied with the amount, she gently wrapped her hand with multiple yarrow leaves. She was annoyed with Oleander's comment, and it showed in the harshness while doctoring her hand. How could he be sarcastic at a time when they really could be surrounded by vampires? The scent of her blood could draw them in. She trembled at the thought.

"Good as new," Strelitzia said, sighing with temporary relief. Her voice gave away her sense of fear.

"Do we have to go in there?" Rosebud asked, with Crocus standing on edge now on her shoulder. He looked like he was ready to burn someone alive.

This made Strelitzia wonder what dragon-fly fire would do to a vampire. Considering his small size, he had a rather large flame, but it was still nothing compared to that of a normal-sized, adult dragon.

"Yes, unfortunately. Just stay close. Between Oleander and Crocus, you will be the safest a goblin has ever been." Strelitzia placed her hand on Rosebud's other shoulder and smiled at her.

Strelitzia feared more than anything what would happen to this small goblin. Would she become a snack for a vampire? Would she be left on her own? She tried to push these thoughts away by focusing on Oleander and Crocus, and the ways they'd be able to potentially save them all. Oleander was the grandest warrior Lumiara had ever seen. Crocus, a feisty dragon-fly who was not afraid to use his fire. Between the two of them, they'd be ok.

"Let's get this over with. I can already tell this forest is going to wreak havoc on my nervous system." Oleander said.

Strelitzia felt awful for Oleander. She could only imagine what his warrior training had been like and how his brain now reacts to these types of situations. He had never been to war, but she still wondered at the toll all the training took on the warriors. They had to be prepared for anything at any given moment. How does one find rest like that?

"Oleander," Strelitzia called to him. "Thank you. For everything. You have no idea how happy it made me that you agreed to come along. I've never felt safer." She said the words both to attempt to put Oleander in a better mindset, but also because she felt she needed to tell him how she felt.

She reached up and wrapped her arms around his neck, hugging him tightly. When he wrapped his arms around her waist, she felt the safest she ever had. She gently kissed his cheek before releasing him. When she looked up at him, Oleander was smiling, just barely, but it was there.

The longer Strelitzia was with Oleander, the more she never wanted to spend a moment apart from him. She started to wonder how this would make her parents feel. If she chose a lower-class warrior as her mate. Would he be welcomed with open arms, or would he be shunned and deemed unworthy? Did her parents even have that choice? Once she made her selection, were her parents allowed to say no? There were too many questions surrounding this thought. Strelitzia pushed them away to focus on their current situation. A situation she could potentially control.

"What was that? Did you see that?" Rosebud announced, as she pointed toward what looked to have once been a fortress.

"See what?" Oleander asked as he slowly got his trusty knife out.

"I think there's someone over there," Rosebud continued, her voice quivering.

"I don't think there's anyone here. This place looks completely deserted," Strelitzia said as she strained to see through and around the distant ruins.

"You and Crocus stay here. Strelitzia and me will go check it out. Crocus, you don't let anything happen to Rosebud, okay?" Crocus stood at attention and saluted Oleander.

"Strelitzia and I." Oleander shifted his attention, now confused.

"What?" Strelitzia gazed at him with compassion. He really didn't know proper grammar.

"It's not Strelitzia and me, it's Strelitzia and I." Strelitzia didn't fully understand why she had even felt the need to correct him. Especially now.

She knew he would need to work on these small things if she wanted him to be her king. But why now? Was it because she was nervous? Was it a way to deflect from their current situation? Was she really so focused on their possible marriage that she ignored the dangers around them?

"Why do I need to know that? What's the difference anyway?" Oleander sounded annoyed or maybe confused; either way, Strelitzia dropped it, not wanting him to lose his focus.

"Never mind. It doesn't matter." Strelitzia knew what her heart desired, but Oleander would need training in doing things properly before she could have what she wanted.

"We'll be right back," Strelitzia told Rosebud. "Here," she handed her grandmother's knife to the young goblin. "This knife will protect you. Hold it close and use it if you must."

Rosebud carefully took the knife and smiled up at Strelitzia, a silent thank you from an adolescent goblin. Strelitzia smiled back and gently put a hand on Rosebud's cheek before returning to Oleander's side and making their way to the ruins. The decrepit ruins that Strelitzia assumed were hunting grounds for bloodthirsty vampires.

Chapter Sixteen

The Everthorne Vampire

Strelitzia and Oleander moved slowly towards the ruins. Strelitzia took glances back at Rosebud and Crocus every couple of steps, to ensure to herself that they were okay.

As they got closer, Strelitzia felt a sharp gust of wind pass her. She froze as her arms gradually lined with goosebumps, and the hair on the back of her neck stood. Slowly, Strelitzia glanced around, but she didn't see anything. The wind was howling quietly as it blew through the ruins. The ocean's waves crashed onto the shore like they wanted revenge, taking the demolished dock back with it, piece by piece. The gloom that lingered in the air was making Strelitzia feel uneasy. She remained close to Oleander, the only thing that gave her bravery.

"What's wrong?" Oleander whispered to her.

"I don't know. I thought I felt something." Low laughter erupted from somewhere within the ruins, which made Oleander and Strelitzia pull their weapons.

"Strelitzia, if we make it out of this, remind me to be mad at you for a couple of days." Strelitzia nodded.

"Valid request," Strelitzia said as a nervous giggle escaped her throat. "I wouldn't be happy with myself if I were in your position."

Once they got to the center of the ruins, Strelitzia dropped her arms to her sides and gazed in amazement at the sight around her. The tall stone pillars, which had started to crumble, and the surrounding walls held memories that she could almost see. There were remnants of a marble floor beneath their feet and a large doorway; the physical door had since been ripped off its hinges and lay in pieces.

"This is amazing," Strelitzia announced.

"Only a goblin would think ruins are amazing." Strelitzia and Oleander whipped around at the sound of the male voice, but no one was there.

"Dang it, Strelitzia!" Oleander exclaimed while turning in circles.

Strelitzia knew Oleander was upset; she could see it on his face, hear it in his voice, and could absolutely not blame him. She had no idea who was here, but she feared it was a vampire. One who was playing with its food.

"Just wait. Let me try something." Strelitzia put her hand on Oleander's chest, moving as close to him as she could, an attempt to calm both his nerves and hers.

Being this close to Oleander brought back that warmth in her heart. His scent almost made her forget what they were doing. She refocused quickly, trying to hold her breath to eliminate the distraction of Oleander's smell.

"Hello? We're a bit lost. We're trying to get to Heedmore. Would you show yourself so we may ask for directions? We mean no harm." Strelitzia attempted to sound less royal than she actually was, while also sounding educated. She had read that vampires were extremely intelligent and proper beings.

"Harm? Come now, young royal goblin. Do you really think a posh little girl like yourself could harm a vampire?" The laughter continued, sending a chill down Strelitzia's spine.

Strelitzia gripped her knife harder, applying pressure to the wound on her palm, causing fresh blood to ooze out of it, soaking through her bandage. It stung, but she paid it no mind. How did he know that she was royal? The thought that this vampire knew who she was spooked Strelitzia, but it also made her angry. Her fear slowly started to shift to rage. This vampire was toying with her, and she was not a fan.

"Please, we only seek advice and direction." Strelitzia tried again to speak to the mystery man hiding among the ruins.

She and Oleander stood back to back and continued making small circles. Her heart pounded in her chest with fear. Not only for herself, but for Oleander. She then remembered Rosebud and Crocus were also sitting nearby, and her worry grew. She took a quick glance towards them, just to prove to herself that they were ok.

"And why would two young goblins need to go to Heedmore?" the voice chuckled, sounding like the question was more a statement than demanding answers. "But, the bigger question is, why are you at Bloodmist Cove?"

"Why don't you show yourself so we can speak face to face?" Strelitzia practically demanded.

All fear had left her body, and she was filled with an anger she'd never known. The authority in her voice strongly reminded her of her mother's. This gave her a small sense of pride. The vampire emerged but remained in the shadows. Strelitzia saw the silhouette of his body, and he looked put together. Not a single hair was out of place, at least that she could see. The wind was still whirling through the ruins, making her hair blow, but everything about this vampire stayed perfectly still.

"We are looking for an Everthorne vampire. I was told their vampire venom is the strongest, and I wish to barter some. I had read that the remaining Everthorne vampire resided in Heedmore and thought this would be the best way to get there unnoticed." Strelitzia announced to the shadowy figure.

Strelitzia watched as the vampire took small, casual steps towards her and Oleander.

"I don't like this Strelitzia," Oleander whispered in her ear.

Strelitzia turned to Oleander and gazed deeply into his eyes. There was a chance they would die, here and now, which scared her more than anything.

"I love you. I think I always have." Strelitzia whispered back to Oleander. She watched Oleander's eyes widen, and his jaw drop open.

"I don't think now is the time for this," Oleander replied, sounding very anxious.

Strelitzia opened her mouth to speak, but before she could, the vampire appeared directly in front of them. Strelitzia and Oleander stood stunned. Oleander had his knife ready and waiting.

"I find it very disrespectful to respond to a princess that way. Don't you?" The vampire aimed his question at Oleander.

How did he hear that? How did he know that she was a princess? Strelitzia grew nervous. What else could this vampire do? She cursed herself for not studying vampires further before leaving on this adventure.

Strelitzia took a good look at the vampire standing before them; his sharp teeth gleamed, sending a wave of nerves coursing through her. He was tall and muscular with long, wavy, golden hair, high cheekbones, and a sharp jawline. With his obvious quickness, this vampire could kill them within a mere second. The thought made her mouth go dry.

"What makes you think I'm a princess?" Strelitzia asked the vampire. Her voice was hoarse and trembled slightly, and she hated herself for it. She didn't want to show this vampire that she was scared.

"I'm not in the mood for games, and I have another matter to attend. So, *princess*, shall we continue?" Strelitzia didn't know how to take this.

"Can you help us?" Oleander chimed in.

Strelitzia could hear the annoyance in his voice at the vampire's tactics, and she wished he would calm down. If they remained calm, they wouldn't die. Hopefully. Strelitzia's palm ached as she continued squeezing her knife. She only then remembered that she was bleeding. Her heart skipped at the realization as she attempted to keep her eyes from widening.

This vampire could smell her. Royal blood was no different from the lower-class blood, at least not that she was aware.

"Your blood smells familiar, young goblin. Care to share who you really are?" The vampire asked, causing Strelitzia to panic.

"My name is Strelitzia." She finally said, while attempting to add confidence to her voice.

She wasn't ashamed of who she was, but she also didn't want to let on that she was royal. Even though this vampire was already assuming she was, she didn't want to let him know that he was right.

"A name is just that—a name. You're hiding something. You wouldn't be related to any elder goblins, would you?" Strelitzia didn't know where he was going with this, but she also wasn't about to tell him about her line of lineage to Gibbous.

"No." She said it curtly.

The vampire laughed. "A quick education, young one. Your pulse quickens when you lie, and I hate lies." Strelitzia gulped down her fear as the vampire was suddenly mere inches from her face, holding her wrist in his cold hands. He sniffed her palm, then a coy grin spread across his face. "Well, this was unexpected. King Gibbous's blood courses through your veins."

Strelitzia froze as the vampire dug inside his coat pocket and pulled out a tiny bottle of swirling green liquid with silver flakes floating gracefully within. Still holding Strelitzia's wrist, he popped the cork and allowed the elixir to pool over her wound. It burned and hissed, yet a gentle smell of her home came rushing to her nose. When Strelitzia looked at the wound, it was like it had never existed. The vampire grinned. "A simple potion to honor King Gibbous."

The realization of which goblin he had been referring to before hit her like a falling boulder. He had met Gibbous in his glory days. Strelitzia's mind started running wild on whether this was a good thing or a bad thing. What happened between this vampire and Master Gibbous? There was nothing in any book about Gibbous encountering a vampire. Strelitzia's thoughts confused her relentlessly, as the fear of her current position grew.

"*Master* Gibbous now. He has not been King for quite some time." Strelitzia corrected him and almost immediately regretted it, scrunching her nose. How could she be so naive as to correct a bloodthirsty parasite? "I'm sorry, I feel I have disrespected you. Please forgive me. What is your name?"

The vampire grinned cynically, his fangs sharp and menacing. "Nothing to forgive." He nodded his head. "I'm Nash Everthorne."

Chapter Seventeen

Vampire Venom

Strelitzia's mouth dropped. She had done it. She found the Everthorne vampire. A flash of hope wormed its way through Strelitzia's brain. Nash Everthorne stood before her, looking as though he were contemplating what he had just heard. Strelitzia worried that he would be angry with her. She listened to the sounds of the angry ocean, not taking her eyes off the vampire. The waves continued their assault on the shores of Bloodmist Cove, sending gusts of chilling wind pounding at the ruins. Strelitzia's hair whipped back and forth, as did her cloak. She glanced back at Rosebud and Crocus, holding her hair in place. Rosebud stood facing her and Oleander, knife drawn and ready. Crocus was standing on the ground in front of Rosebud, wings out and mouth open. She could see the beginnings of his flame ready to leave his throat. She hoped it wouldn't be necessary for them to intervene, but she couldn't know that for sure.

Waiting for the vampire to speak again seemed to last forever. Strelitzia grew more nervous the longer the silence continued. She tried to study the vampire's expression, but he showed nothing.

"So the old goblin still lives. Fascinating. He must have enjoyed my venom." Nash chuckled to himself; he looked lost in a memory. "When I first met Gibbous, he was a newly crowned king, and the goblins were desperate to expand, which is why he journeyed to my land. He discovered vampire venom and wanted some for himself. I wanted something in exchange. I wanted the power of the white crystals, or as we call them, ice crystals. Once he returned with what I desired, we struck an accord; one that would bind us for a lifetime and many more... it would seem." The words flowed out of Nash's mouth like silk.

"You knew Gibbous when he was king?" Strelitzia was bewildered.

How old was this vampire? And why were there no other Everthornes? She assumed they had children as the goblins did; had he never had any? The thought was odd to Strelitzia. He was a good-looking vampire, as far as she knew, and she assumed he wouldn't have a hard time finding a mate. So why hadn't he?

Nash let out an exasperated sigh, "Goblins have the attention span of a gnat." He pinched the bridge of his nose and sighed deeply again.

Strelitzia wondered if that's what all creatures thought about goblins: that they were greedy and had no attention span. She raised an eyebrow at him in disbelief that he could be so rude. Although, she also wasn't entirely sure why she was surprised. She hadn't exactly been nice to him. It started to feel as though all her royal training had gone out the window.

"My apologies." Nash continued, "Yes. As I said, I struck an accord with him when he was a new king, and because he landed a surplus of our vast supply of ice crystals, your people were able to expand into a great nation. My arrangement with him continues, but you knew nothing about it, so I'm curious as to why you need such a coveted vial of my venom?"

Strelitzia thought about how she should answer this. She could lie, but apparently, he would know immediately. Where was the harm in telling him the truth? She sighed, resigning herself to the truth.

"I wish to allow my dragon-fly, Crocus, to speak for extended periods of time. As it is now, the potion I created only works for a couple of hours."

It was Nash's turn to raise an eyebrow at Strelitzia, and she feared he wouldn't hand over the venom for such a silly reason. What did he care if Crocus could talk? Crocus flew his way up and landed on Strelitzia's shoulder, showing off his impressive wings.

"Dragon-flies are vile little creatures. Why do you allow one to follow you around and perch its grimy claws on your shoulder?" Strelitzia's mouth dropped.

"Dragon-flies are not vile. We treated them with respect, gave them treats, food, and shelter, and they have been loyal. Crocus is one of my very best friends. Just because your kind don't see the use in them doesn't mean we don't. His fire helps us, he cheers me up when I need him to, and he never lets me tackle anything alone. He is a valuable part of my life."

Strelitzia could feel Crocus puff a little bigger as she gently reached up and patted his head.

"Interesting. Well, knowing the time, if I don't return soon, my wife will kill me… well, if I weren't already dead." He snickered to himself. "To honor your bloodline." Nash pulled out a bottle from his satchel and extended it to Strelitzia.

Strelitzia glared at the small vial that Nash had just handed her, and it was everything she'd read about. The thick, green liquid looked majestic as the silver flakes floated in the bottle. They swirled and dazzled, shining with each movement. Like shooting stars across a midnight sky. She smiled.

"Thank…" Strelitzia glanced around, hoping she'd be able to give Nash a proper thank you, but he was gone.

"Man, they move really fast," Oleander commented. "You got what you came for, though. The real thing, at that." Strelitzia looked up at Oleander, and he was smiling down at her.

The vampire disappearing so suddenly only left her with more questions. She wanted to know more about the vampires since everything she had read had been proven to be just a made-up story by goblins who didn't actually know any better. Or maybe Nash was different. Maybe the other vampires do resemble the old goblin tales. Maybe, thanks to King Gibbous, she was one of the lucky ones who had an overall pleasant encounter with the blood thirsty undead.

Chapter Eighteen

Journey Home

"Are you ready to try this out, Crocus?" Strelitzia asked after they'd gotten into open water, heading back to Lumiara. Crocus casually made his way over to Strelitzia, which concerned her. She had assumed he'd be jumping for joy. Strelitzia glanced over at Oleander, a concerned expression on her face. Oleander shrugged.

She removed the delicate glass lid of the tiny vial and was hit with a strong scent of cooked meats, rosemary, and thyme. It smelled delicious, good enough to eat. She took out her own vial, popped the cork, and slowly started pouring a small amount into the vampire venom. She watched as the green and silver battled her own lime green for dominance in the small glass until it was perfectly combined. She lowered the bottle down to Crocus, who stuck his nose in gingerly.

Strelitzia, Oleander, and Rosebud waited impatiently for Crocus to start chatting.

Crocus gave a small shake, like he was trying to get water off his wings, and Strelitzia watched as his eyes widened and a smile spread across his miniature face.

"This stuff smells great! Don't you think it smells great? I think it smells wonderful! It makes me feel all tingly inside. Is it supposed to do that? How long does this stuff last now that it's mixed with venom? Am I going to turn into a vampire? Is there vampire blood in here? I don't want to live off drinking blood! The taste is awful. That metallic taste, bleh. No, thank you!" There he was. The Crocus that Strelitzia had grown to love. The talkative, playful, curious Crocus. She smiled as he continued, hoping that this would work.

"How do you feel, Crocus?" Rosebud asked him with excitement filling her voice.

"I feel great. How do you feel?" Rosebud laughed, which made Strelitzia's smile widen.

Strelitzia watched as Crocus and Rosebud enjoyed an in-depth conversation about their journey, the people they met, the places they went, and the memories they would cherish. While in a mesmerized state, Strelitzia shrieked as Oleander put his arm around her shoulders.

"Sorry." He said, not letting her go. "I didn't mean to startle you."

"It's okay," Strelitzia replied, her heart rate returning to normal. "I guess I was just lost in the moment. Hey, I actually wanted to talk to you about something." Oleander let go of Strelitzia's shoulders and faced her, allowing Strelitzia to take a good look at him in the gleaming sun. He was really very attractive. He had grown into quite a goblin specimen from the young goblin she had grown up with. She hoped, silently, that he would agree with what she was about to suggest.

"What's up?" He asked her, and her heart skipped a beat.

Strelitzia toyed with her cloak, trying to find the bravery to talk to him about her plan.

"I was wondering if you had ever considered joining the royal family?" Strelitzia held her breath waiting for his response.

The look on his face told her that he hadn't and that he was confused by the question.

"Me? Royal? No. Never would've thought of that. I'm a warrior. I wasn't trained in royal protocols or mannerisms. I'm just a brute warrior. Why?" Strelitzia didn't know how to take this information.

Surely, he had thought about a life with her. Had he expected that they would live happily ever after with the rest of the lower class? That was out of the question for her. She was the only princess; if she didn't remain within the royal family, the Lýsa Crystal's gifts would, potentially, vanish.

"Well, if you *were* presented the opportunity to be a royal, would you take it?" Strelitzia remained hopeful that he would say yes, but there was a nagging feeling in her gut that he wanted nothing to do with being royal. Not that she could ever blame him.

"I don't know. I guess I would have to think about it. That's a lot of responsibility that I don't know if I'd be up for. I'm a simpleton, Strelitzia, not royalty." Strelitzia's soul was crushed.

In his entire response, all she heard was no. She felt as though the world was crashing in around her. What was she to do now? She'd have to choose a king when she returned home; otherwise, her father would be even more cross with her than he probably already is.

"Alright. I was just curious." Strelitzia tried to smile with defeat looming in her heart. She ended the conversation with Oleander and refocused on the fun that Crocus and Rosebud were having.

Sailing home was much less eventful than it had been getting to Thornveil Isle. The ocean was calm, Hafgufa was nowhere in sight, and it was peaceful. Strelitzia stared off the side of the boat, taking mental pictures of her surroundings. Birds tangoed with the clouds, singing as they flew. The refreshing breeze that flowed through Strelitzia's hair. The way the ocean swayed gracefully in tune with the wind. How the sunlight danced on its surface. The way ripples formed when tiny fish jumped out and back into the water. Above all, the smell of the salt water. She wanted to remember this forever.

"Land!" Strelitzia heard Rosebud yell, breaking her trance.

"It's only been a day," Strelitzia said to Oleander, shocked that land was so close. "How have we journeyed across the water in such a short amount of time?" Oleander shrugged.

"I'm not really sure, but I'm not going to complain about it."

Strelitzia didn't want to complain either, but suspicion grew. She felt uneasy having made such a long journey in less than a full day.

Strelitzia glanced toward the shore, hoping they weren't being met by the fae. They had bartered safe passage before and hoped that it still stood for their journey back home. She saw the path that she had created before they left and was glad that it was still there. The boat got closer and closer, and she didn't see any sign of danger. She took a deep breath and hoped for the best.

The boat reached the shore and slowly came to a stop just on the sandbank. Oleander and Crocus got off the boat first, Strelitzia and Rosebud followed. No sooner did Rosebud's feet touch the sand, the boat began to rumble. Strelitzia turned and watched as the vines unraveled and shot into the ground. She dodged pieces of large redwoods that flew back to wherever they'd originally come, until all that was left was the sail they had made.

"Well, that was weird," Oleander announced. Strelitzia agreed.

They turned and started their walk through Nebraria with no interruption. Strelitzia glanced back after a while and noticed that their path was disappearing. The ground that had been stripped was covering itself back up with grass, like being covered with a warm blanket at bedtime. No one would ever know they had been here. Strelitzia smiled at the thought and silently thanked the earth and the green crystal for assisting in keeping her secret.

Chapter Nineteen

The Announcement

After an easy trip home, Strelitzia got little Rosebud back safely to her parents. They weren't nearly as upset as she thought they should've been. It was almost like they hadn't even noticed she was gone. Strelitzia felt confused and worried for Rosebud. What kind of life must she be living if her parents hadn't even noticed she was gone? She was always so happy and free whenever Strelitzia saw her, but now she wondered what other horrors she was dealing with at home.

"Well, I guess this is goodbye for now. I hope your father isn't too cross with you." Oleander said to Strelitzia.

"I don't think he will be. I can handle his rage if he is. Will you be attending the announcement ceremony? I believe my father will rush me to do it and get it over with." Strelitzia laughed just slightly.

"I wouldn't miss it. As long as I'm not thrown in jail before then anyway." Oleander laughed along with her.

"You won't be, I'll make sure of that. No one will go against the wishes of the future Queen. I hope you won't worry." Strelitzia smiled at Oleander sincerely.

Oleander leaned down and wrapped Strelitzia in a hug. She took a deep breath, wanting to remember how it felt to be in his arms, in the chance that she'd never feel it again. She wanted to remember how he smelled like home and safety. After he released her, Strelitzia stared into his eyes and hoped that her plan would go off without a hitch. As they parted ways, Strelitzia felt a strain in her heart. She didn't like the thought of not spending her days with Oleander. He made her feel safe, seen, and loved. Watching him walk away from her was torture.

When she opened the door to her home, she was faced by her parents. They were sitting on their stone couch, watching the fire. Each holding a goblet of tea.

"Oh, Strelitzia!" Her mother yelled as she raced over to her. "I've missed you so. Please tell us of your adventure." Strelitzia was confused as her mother guided her to the couch. Neither of them were yelling.

"You're not mad?" She asked.

"I was at first." Her father started. "But your mother explained to me that we needed to let you do this and that you left with her blessing. I can't argue with your mother. She's very persuasive." The King laughed as he hugged his Queen.

"However, now you must name a husband. Everything was put on standby for when you decided to return. We will have the ceremony tomorrow."

"Yes, father."

"I trust you have someone in mind?" Strelitzia smiled at her mother's question.

"I do."

The next day, all the goblins gathered in the great hall within the largest of the mountains in Lumiara, for a second time. The room was buzzing with worry as King Verdant and Queen Moonglade once again took their places on the royal redwood thrones.

The King escorted his Queen with pride as they walked arm in arm. Their moss and flower-covered robes trailed behind them. He assisted her into her chair before taking a seat of his own. Just like he had before, and every other time he entered this room. Princess Strelitzia, full of nerves, took her seat on her father's left. She fidgeted with her fingers, hoping this would be a happy ending.

The King rose, ready to speak to his clan. "Welcome back. Today, we again ask my daughter who she has chosen to be her King. I trust that my daughter, having gone on her own adventure, has now made her selection." He paused and looked over at Strelitzia, smiling, "Today, hopefully, we will please the Lýsa Crystal with the promise of the next marriage of royalty. Ensuring our clan's future and the continuation of the gifts we receive. Everyone, my beautiful daughter, Princess Strelitzia." Strelitzia took a deep breath to calm her nerves before standing and facing the entirety of the goblin settlement.

She stood in awe at the crowd before her. They had once been a small settlement of merely one hundred goblins. That number had grown to the thousands. She wondered if this speech was easier in earlier days with fewer eyes staring at you.

"Hello," she paused to steady her shaking voice, "I'd like to start by thanking each of you for your patience with me. I know I gave all of you quite a fright last time I stood here before you." Strelitzia glanced around the room. She started to panic when she couldn't find Oleander. He had said he'd be here. Where was he? Her palms became clammy as a lump in her throat formed. What if he wasn't here? She took a deep breath and fought away the tears that were beginning to form in her eyes.

"I have chosen who I wish to spend my days with. This goblin has shown me what it truly means to care for another. To keep them safe and ensure they feel loved. I only hope that he agrees to my proposal." The crowd started to whisper among themselves.

Strelitzia was her father a second time around. No one had known that he would choose Moonglade to be his queen. Now, no one knew who Strelitzia had decided on. Momentum grew as she paused to steady herself once again. She felt a tear slide down her cheek out of fear.

"I choose the most renowned warrior in our settlement, Oleander." The crowd gasped while Strelitzia's heart raced.

No royal had ever chosen anyone from the lower class before. Always the superior class. The goblins that were directly beneath the royals.

Strelitzia stood, waiting, losing hope with every second that ticked by, until finally, she saw him. Her heart skipped a beat as she watched Oleander make his way towards the front of the crowd. She watched with a full heart as the crowd parted to let him through. Each goblin he passed stared at him with wonder.

"Strelitzia, are you sure?" Her father had appeared behind her and whispered in her ear.

"Absolutely." Strelitzia couldn't dim her smile if she tried.

Oleander walked onto the stage and grasped Strelitzia's hands. Strelitzia froze. He didn't look happy. In fact, he almost looked angry.

"Is this why you asked me that question about being a royal?" He asked her.

"Yes. Are you angry?" Strelitzia's smile vanished as concern took over her senses. She was terrified of being denied in front of the entire settlement.

"I could never really be angry with you. I've loved you since we were young. I never thought that being with you would be an option." Oleander's words sent Strelitzia into a tailspin.

"So, do you accept?"

"I do," Oleander said, loud enough to echo through the room, and he smiled broadly, melting Strelitzia's heart.

Strelitzia jumped up and wrapped her arms around his neck, hugging him tightly. She felt secure, wrapped in Oleander's strong arms as he lifted her off the ground, twirling them both around. When he placed her back on the ground, he cupped her face, leaned in, and kissed her. In front of everyone.

The crowd erupted in cheers at the sight before them. The only heir had finally chosen her husband; the Lýsa Crystal's gifts would continue. Securing the goblins' safety for another generation.

King Verdant rose and stood between Oleander and Strelitzia. He shook Oleander's hand and hugged his daughter.

"My good goblins," The King spoke, and the crowd hushed. "We welcome Sir Oleander, our top warrior, into the royal family. From this moment forward, he will be the head of our military, and I could not be prouder of my daughter's selection. Please join me in congratulations to Princess Strelitzia and Sir Oleander."

The crowd cheered on as Strelitzia gazed into Oleander's eyes.

Chapter Twenty

Returning the Crystal

The wedding was everything Strelitzia didn't know she had dreamed of. She had never been one of those girls to daydream about their wedding day, but the day had been perfect. Strelitzia wore a lilac colored, floor-length dress that had been made from silk that was harvested from silkworms. The skirt of the dress was covered with jasmine and deep purple wisteria flowers that were secured at the waist of the dress. She wore a crown made of vines with the same flowers as the skirt of her dress, sprinkled with gold dust. Oleander had been fitted in an off-white silk suit with a linen shirt that had been delicately made with flax plant fibers. Strelitzia loved how they made their clothes in Lumiara. Everything was provided by the nature that protected them.

The wedding was held in the ceremony room, and all the goblins were present. What Strelitzia hadn't been able to predict was who would be leading the ceremony. As she walked down the aisle with her father, she froze. She saw Oleander standing stoically next to Master Gibbous.

"Father," Strelitzia whispered, "How is Master Gibbous here? Why isn't he in his tree?"

"Honestly, my child, no one knows. He just showed up and said he would be performing the nuptials today." Strelitzia smiled, thinking that the Lýsa Crystal or the vampire venom had something to do with this.

Master Gibbous stood with a cane and had a long moss cloak that covered his body and part of the floor. His face was exactly as she had seen it in the tree, bark colored with many wrinkles and a long, white beard. His eyes looked soft and full of joy.

As King Verdant escorted his daughter down the aisle, Strelitzia saw little Rosebud in the crowd, with Crocus resting on her shoulder. It made Strelitzia smile seeing the two of them together. As they reached the front of the aisle, Queen Moonglade wrapped Strelitzia in a warm hug before releasing her to her next journey. When she reached the front, she curtsied to Master Gibbous and smiled before turning her attention to her soon-to-be husband.

"My dear goblins," Master Gibbous started before he was hit with a fit of coughing, "Excuse me, it's been a while." The crowd softly laughed. "We are gathered today to join Princess Strelitzia and Sir Oleander in marriage. To protect the settlement's gifts from the Lýsa Crystal and its guidance. Princess Strelitzia and I have a connection that does not happen often within our settlement. My own blood runs through her veins. She is an extension of me, which gives me great joy and hope for our settlement. The Lýsa Crystal has granted me this one last gift before my transition to the earth is complete. I've spent hundreds of years in my tree and have enjoyed witnessing all the generations of goblins flourish." Strelitzia's eyes shot to Gibbous. What did it mean? There was concern and worry buried deep in her purple eyes. Did that mean after this, he'd be gone forever? He'd finally move on to the other side. She wasn't sure she was ready for that.

"Oleander, do you promise to love and protect Strelitzia, to guide her in her darkest days, to be a listening ear and a shoulder to lean on?" Master Gibbous continued.

"Absolutely," Oleander said. All the goblins giggled, as did Strelitzia. Master Gibbous smiled.

"Strelitzia, do you promise to love and support Oleander, to advise him when he's rash, to carry his children and build a steady home?"

"I do." Strelitzia's smile was contagious as she made her promise to Oleander.

Master Gibbous wrapped a long twine around Oleander and Strelitzia's held hands. He then laid his own hand on top of theirs. As he did, the purest white roses began to bloom. Strelitzia's eyes sparkled in amazement, and she wondered if he had a green crystal hidden somewhere within his robes.

"With the powers vested in me, the powers of Maker and the gifts of the Lýsa Crystal, I present to you, for the first time, King Oleander and Queen Strelitzia." Oleander leaned in and kissed Strelitzia, sealing their promises to each other.

It dawned on Strelitzia that she hadn't returned the green crystal yet, and she hoped that the Lýsa Crystal wouldn't be angry with her. It had only been a couple of days, so she was hopeful that it wouldn't.

"Oleander, I need to go see the Lýsa Crystal," Strelitzia whispered to him as they made their way back up the aisle. All the goblins were cheering for them as they passed.

"Then let's go." He replied.

Strelitzia and Oleander quietly made their way down the dark hall that led to the Lýsa Crystal. The familiar light blue glow weaved its way around them. They followed the stream carefully all the way to the glowing Lýsa Crystal. Strelitzia glanced down at the water and smiled, seeing the reflections of all the colored crystals. Strelitzia continued walking, leaving Oleander at the entrance, until she met the dirt that the Lýsa Crystal rested on. She knelt before the Lýsa Crystal, removing the green crystal from a pocket she had added to her wedding dress.

"Dearest Lýsa Crystal. I feel I have so much to thank you for. I wish to thank you for the protection that the green crystal provided. Without its help, I don't believe we would've completed our journey. I also need to deeply thank you for allowing Master Gibbous out of his tree to attend our wedding. Your gifts are greatly appreciated." Strelitzia kissed the green crystal and the small shard before placing them on the dirt in front of the massive Lýsa Crystal.

Strelitzia looked up and, for the first time, saw her reflection staring back at her. The Lýsa Crystal had never been like a mirror, but she smiled. Somehow knowing that this was a good thing.

The ground began to rumble as roots slowly made their way out of the ground. She watched as they grasped the green crystal and dragged it back underground. One stray root remained. Slowly, it wrapped itself around her wrist, giving her a gentle squeeze. Strelitzia smiled as she then watched the root return to its underground resting place. Strelitzia wondered when the next time anyone would see a green crystal. She stood, not taking her eyes off the Lýsa Crystal. Being around the Lýsa Crystal made Strelitzia feel a sense of peace. She kissed her hand, reached out, and placed it on the Lýsa Crystal.

Thank you, Queen Strelitzia. For honoring your promise.

"It truly is magnificent, isn't it?" Strelitzia jumped and turned around.

Standing next to Oleander, who looked as though he was standing next to the greatest hero in all the realms, eyes wide with a huge, toothy grin, was Master Gibbous.

"Master Gibbous!" Strelitzia said with excitement as she made her way to him. "I'm so glad you were able to be here today, but what does this mean for you now?" Gibbous smiled.

"It means I may finally rest. I know now that our settlement is held by steady hands. Hands trusted not only by the Maker, but by the Lýsa Crystal as well. I was granted leave to remain beyond my time, to linger between ending and beginning, until another like me would walk these grounds. That moment has come. You are that goblin." Strelitzia's jaw dropped.

"Me? There are so many generations between us; how was there no one before me?"

"Let me speak plainly, though the truth is anything but simple. Among goblins, blood is carried forward from one life to the next, thinning with each passing age. In time, mine faded entirely, its echo lost to the world. Yet in you, it stirs again, awakening an era long thought ended. Few are aware of this truth. Fewer still would believe it. You are my reflection, shaped anew, my likeness, not of face, but of spirit. Your longing to cross borders and test the realms is one I remember well, for I was once that goblin, beneath moons far older than these. And as your travels have already begun to teach you, your return has not gone unnoticed. You have given the Lýsa Crystal something it has not known in a very long time, hope." Gibbous explained.

"But how? How do I have your blood?" Strelitzia was confused how Gibbous's blood could come back after being watered down for generations.

"You, my dear, are not merely special, you were chosen. My blood was not passed to you by chance but given as a gift from the Maker Himself. He knew you before your first breath ever touched the living world. He knew you would be the one trusted to carry my line forward, to bear what was lost and make it new again. Now, if you will excuse me." Gibbous slowly walked with his cane towards the Lýsa Crystal.

"Wait!" Strelitzia yelled to him as tears welled in her eyes. "What if I need you?" Gibbous gave her a warm smile.

"I will always be with you. My faith in you is absolute, Strelitzia, unshaken, unwavering. To witness your becoming, to watch you rise into who you are meant to be, has been one of the greatest joys of my existence. Whatever paths you walk, know this: you have never done so unseen." Gibbous turned to the Lýsa Crystal and gently placed his hand on it. "I'm ready." Strelitzia heard Gibbous whisper.

Strelitzia and Oleander watched as the Lýsa Crystal began to glow a bright white. Swirls of glittery white orbited around Gibbous. He was lifted off the ground and spun around to face Strelitzia. Strelitzia's heart ached with the unknown of what was happening. Gibbous smiled at her before closing his eyes.

You have done well, Gibbous. Thank you for keeping me safe. I know Strelitzia will lead where you leave off with great honor. I give you the freedom of peace.

Strelitzia heard the words echo through the room and wondered if Oleander heard them as well. She didn't ask him, though, just kept her watering eyes on Gibbous. The glittery white streams flowed into Gibbous before bursting back out of him. Strelitzia watched as Gibbous slowly disappeared.

Once he was gone, everything went dark. There was no glow from the Lýsa Crystal. No streams of colors from all the crystals lining the walls and ceiling. Just darkness. Strelitzia lowered her head and cried, turning to bury her face in Oleander's chest, knowing that Gibbous was now gone. Amidst her tears, she smiled at the knowledge that Master Gibbous was finally able to reunite with the love of his life, and he would remain unbothered, at peace.

Epilogue

Years Later

Strelitzia strolled through the settlement, interacting with all the goblins, with Crocus on her shoulder. She had decided to visit the settlement as often as she could. Doing this, she had been able to eliminate a lot of conflict between the goblins that had previously gone unknown to the royals. She had learned so much from them and was grateful that they all happily accepted her presence. Rosebud's parents were no longer together, and Rosebud was happier than ever. She had two homes and two happy parents with no arguments or fights. Separating had never been looked kindly upon within the goblin kind; however, Strelitzia realized that at times it truly was for the best and changed the unspoken law. Allowing goblins to separate from their mates to live their happiest lives.

"Princess!" Rosebud yelled as she ran up to Strelitzia. Strelitzia really took Rosebud in. She had grown into such a beautiful goblin over the last couple of years. Her long, flowing, two-toned hair glistened as it swayed, and her eyes seemed to reflect the stars.

"Hey, Rosebud," Strelitzia said as she hugged her. She was amazed at how tall she'd gotten. She was almost as tall as Strelitzia now. "How's everything?"

"Great. I've been working in the garden with my mother all day. She's so happy. She sings again and hums along with the birds. She has more pep in her step, and she smiles all the time." Rosebud said with joy.

"And your father?" Strelitzia worried about this response. She had seen the transition in Rosebud's mother, but her father hadn't been coping as well. She worried about the toll that the separation would have on him.

"He's better. Not quite out of the dark yet, but he's getting there. Just the other day, he and I built a chair together in his workshop. I think his workshop has given him a new purpose. He loves building furniture, and he's been giving the things he makes to other goblins in the settlement. He hopes to make a shop one day." Strelitzia smiled, glad to hear that Rosebud's father had plans and was working towards his happily ever after.

"How are *you* doing?" Rosebud asked Strelitzia.

"I'm good, just wobbling along." They both laughed. Strelitzia said goodbye to Rosebud and watched as she ran off to rejoin her mother.

One thing Strelitzia had done since becoming Queen that she was incredibly proud of was creating a marketplace much like the one she had wandered through while at Crimsonreach Crossing. Goblins had their own booths, and they could all trade with each other the things that they needed but couldn't provide for themselves. They would barter or trade with things more valuable, like coin or their precious trinkets. It brought a fellowship to the settlement that hadn't fully been established before. Some sold food items, some sold clothes, and others sold trinkets. Rosebud's father would be the first with a furniture store front, and Strelitzia was excited to see it.

"I love it in the settlement," Crocus said to Strelitzia as they continued their walk.

"I do too. It's nice down here. How are you feeling?" Strelitzia questioned Crocus.

The vampire venom made it possible for Crocus to speak for days at a time without needing more of her talking potion.

"I feel great!" Crocus chimed.

"Are you getting tired yet?" The one thing Strelitzia hadn't known was that adding the vampire venom did something to Crocus's small body, and when the potion was wearing off, it made him extremely tired.

"Not yet, I think I still have another day or two before that happens," Crocus told her with confidence.

Strelitzia smiled as they made their way back to the royal cave.

When they returned, Crocus ran off to do whatever dragon-flies do in their spare time. He probably went to hunt small vermin, something Strelitzia had always found amusing and helpful. She found Oleander in a large room that had been turned into a meeting room. Before they took over the household, and her parents moved out, this room had just been empty. Warriors and captains surrounded Oleander, while he laid out more ways of protecting their settlement from the other realms. Although there was no immediate threat, Oleander wanted to ensure that no one could enter undetected. Strelitzia smiled, watching him in his element. He had grown from a great warrior into an even greater King.

Strelitzia missed her parents but would visit them often. They relocated to a small cave home just below the royal cave and were thoroughly enjoying their retirement. They had about five more years until their transition to the earth began, and they were determined to make the most of each day. After Strelitzia and Oleander were wed, they were able to step down. It was a bittersweet moment, but she knew her parents deserved the retirement of their dreams and was happy to give it to them. Her mother had started a hobby of making clothes. Moonglade took lessons from lower-class goblins in the settlement, while her father decided he wanted to learn to fish and hunt. He wanted to learn how to skin his own food and how to preserve the hides of what he had killed. The last time Strelitzia had spoken to her father about it, he was beaming with pride in his newly acquired skills.

Strelitzia made her way to the royal chambers and lay down on her bed. She was exhausted from her and Crocus's visit with the other goblins of the settlement. That was to be expected, though. Strelitzia's pregnant belly grew more and more every day. She was overjoyed at the thought of being a mother. She rubbed her belly and sang, feeling her baby kick and twist. She had the feeling her young goblin would be a dancer of some form or another. Oleander was going to be a great dad. All her previous fears about him had gone out the window the day she told him that they were expecting.

Oleander had immediately started to voice all the things he would teach the new goblin. He would teach him or her how to protect themselves most effectively with the least amount of effort. He decided he would also teach them how to dry hides from animals. He didn't want them to be as sheltered as Strelitzia had been, and Strelitzia agreed. She wanted her children to learn real-life skills, not just the royal ones. She hoped that this would become a common theme with future royals.

Strelitzia stared out her window into what she could see of the sky, beyond the treetops. Her life was more than she could've dreamed of, and she wondered why she had been so anxious about choosing a husband, settling down, and becoming queen. At the time, it had all felt like too much, but it wasn't as difficult as she had thought. Maybe her adventure had prepared her more than she cared to admit, or maybe it was just the fears of a young, royal goblin who had never experienced a life outside of her own cave walls.

"Master Gibbous, I hope I've made you proud," Strelitzia spoke to the sky. As she did, a single beam of sunlight broke its way through the clouds and trees and straight into Strelitzia's window, warming her face. Her sign that not only was he proud, but he was watching her, protecting her from above.

AND THEY LIVED
Adventurously
EVER AFTER

<u>A Note from the Author</u>

Goblins and Crystals took me outside of my comfort zone. I wanted to challenge myself with this book, and I definitely did. I want to send a heartfelt thank you to Courtney Denelsbeck for allowing me to participate in this project with this amazing group of women.

I'd also like to give a special thank you to Maegwen Salley-Massie, Sofia Simpson, Courtney Denelsbeck, and Raye Turner for all the help they gave me throughout the writing of this book.

Additionally, this book would not be where it is without my editor, Ramona Mihai. I am so glad I stumbled upon your Instagram page. I cannot recommend her enough.

I'd also like to give my husband a shoutout. He has never read one of my books, but he listens, he gives me ideas, and lets me vent when I'm frustrated. For that alone, I am forever grateful to him.

With love,

C.A. Meadows

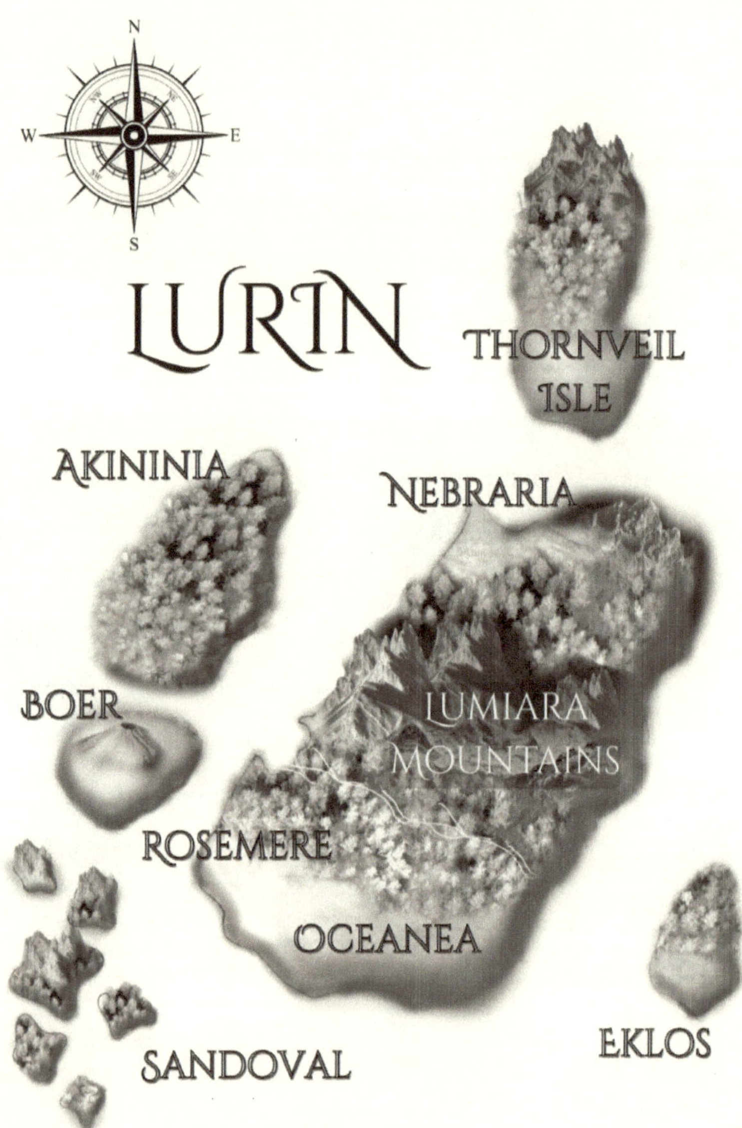
N
NW
W
E
SW
SE
S
LURIN
THORNVEIL
ISLE
AKININIA
NEBRARIA
LUMIARA
MOUNTAINS
BOER
ROSEMERE
OCEANEA
EKLOS
SANDOVAL

For fans of adventurous fantasy with clean romance, Realms of Lurin is a multi-author collection of standalone, regency-inspired, fantasy novellas featuring different magical creatures and set in the same world.

Be sure to check out all the books in the Realms of Lurin Series.

Sirens and Sea Captains by Courtney Denelsbeck

Petals and Poison by Cara Ruegg

Venom and Vows by Maegwen Salley-Massie

Fae and Flames by Sofia Simpson

Goblins and Crystals by C.A. Meadows

Witches and Wolves by Nellie Peters

Tempest and Tiger's Eye by Gabriella Batel

Beaux and Dragons by Candice Pedraza Yamnitz

Goblins & Crystals - C.A. Meadows

About the Author

C.A. Meadows is a Southern California native whose love of storytelling has followed her across the country. A classically trained ballerina from childhood through her teens, she found a new creative outlet in writing after an injury ended her dance career. With an associate's degree and a deep appreciation for literature, art, and history, her stories are shaped by both discipline and imagination.

With a lifelong fascination for astronomy and Greek mythology, particularly the haunting legend of Medusa, C.A. Meadows brings curiosity, discipline, and a touch of darkness to her work. She writes both immersive fantasy and gripping thrillers that border on horror, blending imagination with psychological tension. Her debut novel, Lost in a Nightmare, is the result of years of perseverance after countless drafts left behind. She continues to write with the hope of captivating readers who crave unsettling stories and has many more worlds and nightmares yet to be explored.

Other Books by C.A. Meadows

Fantasies:

Giovanna

Ashlynn

Barbos

Zelvo (Coming 2026)

Thrillers:

Lost in a Nightmare

The Nightmare Returns

The Secret of the Inheritance

For more information, please visit:

Authorcameadows.com

@c.a.meadows on Instagram

9 798999 510970